Silly Heart

~

A. MELCHIONDA

To women who find the strength to leave the men who left them.

Friendship is certainly the finest balm for the pangs of disappointed love.
- Jane Austen

ONE

If I still had a boyfriend, I wouldn't be in this pub tonight. Huh-uh.

There's no way I would be wrapped in Martin Roberts's muscular arms now; he wouldn't be nibbling at my jaw and my head wouldn't be tilted in this unnatural angle that is going to give me a stiff neck in the morning.

"Mmm, you smell of apples, sweetheart," he mumbles.

Oh, God. I wish I could fly away and land softly on my old couch. I'd snuggle up into my fleece blanket, all warm and cozy and watch yet another mind-numbing TV show. Vegetating on my couch: that's what I've been doing pretty much every evening for the last four months.

"Yeah, of apples and cinnamon."

I glance sideways at Martin's flawless face: what's not to like? He's 'the full package,' right here against my clenched fists; that's how my friend Denise described Martin when she persuaded me to go out with one of the young, top-notch executives in her company. And she wasn't lying: Martin is smart, looks like a Nordic god, and smells of expensive cologne. Still, I feel like a snail is climbing up my face. Yuk!

Why can't you just like the guy? I hiss to myself. *Because he is not Nico*, the little voice in my head whispers.

I stifle a groan. I'm a modern, capable woman who can take care of herself. I don't like to feel dependent. Unfortunately, there's a man out there who makes me feel just like that. I've been trying to get him out of my head, but he's always at the back of my mind. My girlfriends would never say it to my face, but I know what they think: that I'm obsessed with Nico.

Maybe I should just admit my fixation with a man that I want desperately but I can't have. My passion for him is a vicious beast that pushes me around 24/7 and won't allow me to consider any other man as boyfriend material, even golden boy Martin. At times like now, I find myself wondering if I'll ever be strong enough to move on; I squeeze my eyes shut to block that disturbing thought.

I open my eyes and my gaze lands on the very reason of my insanity: my ex-boyfriend Nico. He's leaning against the bar, sexy as sin. He's wearing a black fitted t-shirt, a black leather jacket, and a deep scowl. Right next to Nico, his best friend Lallo is propped on a stool, nursing a pint.

I just stand there, gaping at them like a rabbit caught in the headlights. Nico's eyes burn a hole in the back of Martin's head; Lallo is also staring at Martin, but I can't read his expression.

A door slams at the back of the pub, shaking me out of my stupor. Oh, God. What are Nico and Lallo doing here, of all places? This is Soho, in London city, for God's sake, not the little town in Italy where the three of us are originally from.

Nico whispers something in Lallo's ear then he pushes away from the wooden counter and swaggers his way through the pub. I hold my breath: I wish a hole would open right under my feet and save me from what I see coming. Gah! Where's my luck when I need it most?

I gently push against Martin's chest.

"What's wrong, sweetheart?" he drawls, and once again I fight the need to snap back that I'm nobody's 'sweetheart.' But what's the point? Martin's eyes are glued to my lips, his hands clasped on my hips. I heave a sigh: could Martin and I be any more disconnected right now?

I take another peek around Martin's shoulder. Nico pins me with his forest green eyes and I know that this is not going to end well.

"Are you all right?" Martin asks, searching my face.

No, I'm not, but this is not Martin's fault. Honestly, I shouldn't have let things get this far tonight; I've never let a guy kiss me on a first date before. Hell, I don't even know how first dates work   first-hand, I mean. Now hold on, let me explain before you decide that I'm a loser.

I have a confession to make: Nico has been my only boyfriend. That's pretty sad for a twenty-five-year-old, I know, but try to put yourself in my shoes: Nico and I grew up together. He was my first crush, my first flirt, my first kiss, my first boyfriend, my first lover…my first and only everything that revolves around the other sex. Until four months ago, when he dumped me 'to pursue his freedom,' we were inseparable.

The thing is, that's in the past now: Nico is not mine anymore. Not mine, not mine, not mine, I chant in my head as he moves closer like a panther on the hunt. My stomach contracts and I let the familiar pain expand to my chest.

"Lisa, what's going on?" Martin asks, pulling my wandering mind back to the pub.

I mirror his frown and rub my forehead. I don't know what possessed me to agree to this date with Martin. Well, the guy chased me for three weeks and Denise went out of her way to endorse him. To cry it out loud, tonight was my first, desperate attempt to move on… I'm blabbing. I can't believe I'm blabbing in my own head. How pathetic.

"I'm so sorry, Martin."

"And you should be." Nico's stern tone hits me like a slap in the face and my eyes dart up. He's towering over me, six feet two inches of unwavering manly glory, damn him. His jaw is set and his stubborn pout makes me feel like a little girl who did something very, very foolish.

My face flames all over again and I automatically disentangle myself from Martin's embrace, my mouth sealed in a tight line. I'm too embarrassed to retort to Nico's scolding right now but apparently Martin doesn't feel so yielding. Oh, did I mention that my date has had a beer or two tonight? Well, I stopped counting after pint number three: I'm not his mother.

"Who the hell are you?" Martin demands.

"I'm Lisa's boyfriend," Nico answers in a dangerously low voice. "And who are *you?*"

"Nico, we are no longer together," I say, skimming my damp palms over the pockets of my jeans. My own words taste bitter in my mouth, but I need to straighten the record. Nico's nostrils flare but I manage to keep my expression flat, I think.

"Lisa, what the hell is going on here?" Martin barks, looking between Nico and me. I hope he's smashed just enough to not notice the way Nico is looking at him: he wouldn't like it one bit.

This is not how I envisioned tonight would go, I mumble to myself. I thread my fingers through my hair and tug at it, looking around the pub. My eyes meet Lallo's across the room and he shakes his head, ever so slightly.

This place is suddenly too crowded for my taste: I need some fresh air. I grab my handbag from the floor.

"Are you leaving?" Martin asks, opening his arms in disbelief. "Are you actually leaving me here like a moron?"

I stare at Martin's red face. I feel terrible about the way things are going down but I'm beyond ready to call it a night and head back to the safe zone of my mini-apartment. I don't belong in Martin's arms, I never will: I felt it when he first put his hands on me two hours ago. But I didn't want to accept it because the reality that I have a hard time moving on after Nico bothers me on too many levels. Maybe my roommate Penelope is right: maybe I really am under Nico's spell. Yes, he has that sort of powerful magnetism about him and if you think I'm exaggerating, well, you've obviously never crossed paths with sweet-boyfriend-turned-bad-boy Nicolas Neri.

"I'm very sorry, Martin. You are a great guy, but I-"

"But she's mine," Nico states matter-of-factly with that rich, deep voice that makes me and thousands of other females shiver. Excitement and rage blend at the base of my throat: how bad is it that my ex's Neanderthal claim on me makes my blood rush in my veins?

Nico takes a long drag of his beer and slams the green bottle down on a nearby table. How I'd love to slap that smirk off his face right now. He would so deserve that: for being so bold, for pushing his way smugly into my life when he no longer has any right to do so, and for looking so devastatingly handsome, even when I'm mad at him.

That's enough: I turn on my heel and all but run for the

door.

"Elisabetta, wait," Nico commands over the noise. Lallo is following right behind him. People look our way curiously. Nico and Lallo are well known in the London music scene: their band, The Lost Souls, plays in clubs around the city. To be honest, Nico wouldn't go unnoticed even if he wasn't the band's front man, not with that face and that body.

I hurry down the stairs. I hear the stomping of Nico's boots behind me; I hope nobody recognized him.

Nico catches up with me at the bottom of the stairs and my skin burns, right where he's clasping my wrist. He tugs gently and searches my eyes: he must read the warning there because he doesn't invite me back to his place, like he's done every time we've met after he broke up with me. He holds the front door for me instead, walks me to the nearby taxi lane, and opens the car door.

"Tu sei mia, per sempre," Nico whispers in my ear. *You are mine forever.* A shiver runs through me, shaking me to the core. I know he knows the effect he has on me, and for that I hate myself just a little bit more right now.

The car door closes with a soft thud. "Mine," Nico mouths from the other side of the glass. I give my address to the taxi driver and look out of the wet window absently. The black shiny cab rolls though Soho's bright nightlife and I let go of the breath I'd been holding, finally allowing all the conflicting emotions of seeing my ex unexpectedly wash over me. I hate that he still affects me so much, but how do you get over twenty years of your life in four months?

An image of Nico and me running barefoot down the hill at my grandma's farm plays behind my eyes; then we would drop down onto the lush, fresh grass to catch our breath. Lallo would pop out from behind one of the fruit trees and tickle my face with a poppy, or a daisy, making me roll in hysterical laughter. Hot tears fall down my face; we were so happy and carefree, what happened to us? Why does it have to be so complicated?

I wipe my cheeks with the back of my hand and take a steadying breath. I can't go on like this: it's just not healthy. I need to shake away this sense of desolation that Nico left behind when he walked away from me; I need to regain control over my life and fall in love with a decent guy. It feels impossible to be with anybody else but Nico, but I'll try to try. Penny says that for every spell in this world there's a counter spell in another, and I've never hoped more that my friend is right.

TWO

I wake up with a pounding headache that I know no painkiller will be able to take away. I push my hair away from my face and sigh in resignation. I drag myself out of bed and under the shower, ignoring my phone's flashing screen. I don't need to look: I know who it is.

I hear a loud knock at the bathroom door and I jump, startled.

"Lisa, come out of that shower! You've been under the running water for twenty minutes. What are you, a fish?" Penny yells through the steam. "Vamos, it's time!"

"I'm comiiing!" I yell back. Penny knows that I hate it when she gets so bossy so why is she being impossible? Hump! And then I remember what my roommate, friend, and amateur witch talked me into doing. I groan under the hot jet. Why did I ever leave my bed this morning?

I hop out of the shower, comb my hair with a few painful jerks, and paddle to my room. I replace my wet towel with a faded track suit bottom and a clean t-shirt, all the way cursing Nico under my breath. This is all his fault!

I tiptoe into the dark living room and warily sit down on the floor opposite to Penny. I've seen her tampering with candles once, but I've never taken part in a 'ritual' before. I guess the darkness is meant to add to the suggestion, but to be honest all I can think about right now is the wax of the candles staining the wooden floor and what the landlord will say.

I've always been rather pragmatic. I guess that's why, after all, I've resolved to take the bull by the horns and adopt a quite practical approach to forgetting Nico: I'm going to try to find a new boyfriend. Penny, the good friend that she is, wants to help, but to say that her means are unconventional is the understatement of the year.

My gaze falls to the pink string of smoke rising from the candle sitting on the floor between us. "Penny, are you sure this is a good idea?"

When I took Penelope in to live with me just over one year

ago, I was delighted to have a Spanish master's law student as a roommate. But I was also fascinated by the exceptional contradiction of rationality and craziness that Penny is: law enforcer by day, aspirant witch by night. Now that she's decided that her supposed witchcraft will improve my love life, I'm not so sure about this magic thing anymore. Thank God she doesn't take her hobby too seriously, at least most of the time.

"This spell could change your life," my friend says. Uh oh. Her black eyes look huge in the candlelight and the little golden pentagram on her neck twinkles. She got it online for a fiver. "It will help you push Nico into a recess at the far back of your mind, and set you free." Oh, yes, please.

Maybe that's what I need: some help from another world because if you leave it to me to find a new man and start a new life, I'm not so sure I'll be able to do that. It's so hard to move on… I just wish Nico wouldn't stomp on every other thought that blossoms in my head, day and night.

I guess the first step to finding someone else would naturally be to go out more, but that's easier said than done. I'm not used to dating and the thought makes me uncomfortable. I actually think I would have some chances on the dating scene if I wanted: guys seem to like me but when they ask me out, I always decline. The only time I didn't, I ended up at the pub with Martin and look what happened…

I tilt my head up to the dark ceiling and close my eyes. I still need to call Denise to apologize for yesterday night. Martin-the-Nordic-god is her colleague and I somehow feel that I let her down for how things ended up. He wasn't my type, but I'm grateful for Denise's effort.

I love my girlfriends for trying to relax Nico's powerful grip on my aching heart. They are really doing their best to support me, each one in her own unique way, like Penny now with her DIY magic.

"I love you, Penny," I say. Her brows arch and disappear under her bangs.

"I love you too, Chica. Don't you worry, we'll get through this together," she says, with a Spanish accent as thick as her shiny black air, but my Italian accent is no better, I guess. So there you go: we are just two Mediterranean girls fending for our future in London and doing magic in our living room. I stifle a chuckle.

Penny tampers with the touch screen of her iPhone and a soft, new age kind of melody fills the room. Even this simple gesture reminds me of Nico: I've turned my phone off because he wouldn't stop calling and texting me this morning. My shoulders slouch in defeat.

"Give me your list. Now," Penny orders.

I produce a creased piece of paper from the pocket of my tracksuit and suddenly feel self-conscious. Maybe I should have used immaculate white paper and my best writing; instead, when Penny asked me to list all the things I hate about Nico, I tore a sheet from an old notepad on impulse and poured a cascade of spiteful words on the yellowish page. It felt liberating when I put down the terrible accusations yesterday but now I feel like my list is not good enough for Penny's attempt at magic. I shake my head to myself: I think I'm losing it.

Penny's eyes narrow as they scan the list. I'm not sure what she's mumbling, but I think she's swearing under her breath.

"Now close your eyes and repeat after me," she demands solemnly. This is so over the top, even for Penny. Despite the giggle bubbling at the base of my throat, the last thing I'd do right now is laugh in my friend's face. She could be out and about, enjoying this incredibly sunny Saturday morning. Instead, she decided to shut the living room curtains, light candles, and burn something that smells like cherry and makes a lot of smoke, just to help me out of my misery. I'm humbled and grateful beyond words; it's just that this ritual thing is so ridiculous. I manage to bite back a laugh, just barely.

"Lisa! Can't you see how very necessary this is? Nico has a spell on you! I doubt he's actually performed a magic spell on your heart but that's even worse. It's a tragedy!"

Penny takes in my bemused expression and sets her lips in a fine line.

"Natural spells, those that people are able to cast on others naturally, effortlessly, are the nastiest kind. They are extremely difficult to break. So I would appreciate if you took this seriously," she says, waving her hands impatiently. "I need your full commitment, otherwise there's no way it'll work!"

"Yes, yes, you're right, I'm sorry," I say quickly. I close my eyes and compose myself. I just hope that none of these candles will reduce us to ashes. With the sense of sight out of the way, the strong cherry smell invades my nostrils completely and I almost cough.

"Very good. Now repeat after me."

I comply diligently, wondering what the hell I'm saying in this unfamiliar language. While I automatically repeat the incomprehensible mantra that Penny is pulling from my lips, an image of Nico and me holding hands pops to life behind my eyes. He's so hot when his tanned skin glows under the sun…

Damn! So much so for putting an effort in this, I can't even get Nico out of my weak mind for two minutes in a row. The problem is that Nico is in every memory I have, good or bad, because until a few months ago, we were always together. Still, my weakness is so pathetic that I'm never going to tell Penny: she would get so mad.

I hear shredding paper noises: I guess my list is gone. But Nico's many faults are forever burned in my head: how he has changed from loving boyfriend to selfish bastard, how he wants me in his bed but not in his life, how he thinks I belong to him but doesn't truly care about me. If only I could remember at all times what a jerk Nicolas Neri is, that would really help me get over him.

"And we are done!" Penny says excitedly, clapping her hands. I open my eyes. She looks like a little girl who has accomplished a huge thing right now, and I'm not going to ruin her mood.

"Ah, thanks, Penny. You know, I feel much better already."

"You do?"

"I do," I lie, bobbing my head.

"You'll see, this counter spell will definitely help you forget Nico."

"Nico who?" I ask in mock surprise.

Penny bursts out laughing and falls on her back, holding her quivering belly.

THREE

It's Saturday night and, for once, I'm thrilled that I won't be spending it on my couch. I'm going out with my girlfriends. Somehow they ditched all previous commitments last minute and decided to join Penny and me at Yoyo, a club in Mayfair.

There are five of us in our little circle: Penny, Denise, Nancy, Monique, and I. We are close friends but we rarely have a girl's night out, because Nancy's married and Denise and Monique are in relationships. Tonight is the exception though and I'm so excited we are getting all together; only Monique can't make it but I'm already planning to catch up with her next week.

Penny and I hop out of our taxi right in front of the club. The girls reserved a table in the private area so we skip the long queue of people waiting outside. A big, grumpy bouncer gives us a once-over and lets us in with a grunt. Phew!

We leave our jackets at the wardrobe and breeze to the VIP area on our very high heels. I glance around: the females in the club are dressed to impress and Penny and I blend in nicely. Thumping music and elaborate lights welcome us as we make our way through the busy dance floor, hand in hand.

My hips start to swing on their own accord. I really like this club. It has a great vibe and it does have some brilliant DJs lined up every weekend. Tonight is going to cost me a fortune in food and drinks, but for once I don't care: I just want to party with my favorite girls and forget all about Nico for a few hours.

Who knows, maybe I'll even meet Mr. Right tonight. Well, I doubt it, but should that ever happen, I guess I'm ready, or at least my 'exterior me' is. One of the things I learned from my mother from an early age is to always try to look at my best when I go out, no matter if it's to buy milk down at the store or for a night out clubbing. And while year after year of practice have helped me perfect my technique, there's something about my present situation that makes me push my chin up and look as good as I can, despite the ache that seems to have taken permanent residence deep in my heart.

It's not easy to keep up appearances but the product of my efforts strokes a secret sense of revenge deep inside of me: because in my heart of hearts, I want Nico to regret his decision to dump me. I want him to feel like the biggest idiot in the world for tossing me away like he did.

"Lisa, you look fabulous! Way to rock the night, girl!" Nancy says over the music, winking at me. At thirty, she's the oldest of our group. She's American and the owner of the beauty salon in central London we all go to when we want to change our hair style, have our nails done, or get a relaxing massage. Nancy inspects my shiny hair, skims her finger over the soft fabric of my low-cut burgundy dress, and I can see that she approves.

"Aww, thanks Nancy, and look at you! I love your hair!"

Nancy threads her manicured hand through her white-blond hair and flashes me a brilliant smile. She's Barbie-gorgeous and she's a fantastic woman: I love her.

"Thanks, sweetie. Now, I heard about your pub disaster. Tell me all about it."

I automatically look Penny's way. She's obviously told Nancy about my debacle with Martin, with details on the embarrassing finale, I'm sure. Penny's in deep conversation with Denise: she's moving her hands fast to emphasize something she's saying.

It doesn't bother me that Penny told Nancy about my disastrous night: we girlfriends share what bothers us and support each other when we are down. I've realized recently, at this time of need, how blessed I am with my girlfriends' friendship and how special and healthy this network of young women is. What would I do without them?

Nancy pops a pistachio into her mouth and I start to give her my version of the epic pub night fail. By the time I'm done, Denise and Penny have joined us to listen to my pitiful story.

"I'm so sorry, Lisa. I shouldn't have pushed you to go out with Martin," Denise says. She looks mortified.

"Oh please, darling, there's nothing to apologize for. I'm

the one who's sorry for the way things went with your colleague. Hopefully this doesn't put you in an awkward position at work."

"Nah, don't worry. He'll probably avoid me in the kitchen for a while but I don't care."

"Well, at least Nico didn't beat him up," Nancy says with wide eyes.

"They didn't fight, but I guess Martin's ego was bruised enough. He's used to have the upper hand with the ladies, you know," Denise says, and fresh guilt builds in my stomach.

"Nico's a bully," Penny says.

"No, he's not," I answer automatically, and three pairs of eyes dart to me. I cast my glance down in defeat.

"Don't worry, sweetie," Nancy says, "it's all right. We've all been there."

My girlfriends nod, even Penny. Their gorgeous faces tell me that at some point, with another man, they've been blinded by love, or passion, or whatever that chain is that is still keeping me bound to Nico. It's in their big eyes that ooze compassion.

"It's going to be fine."

"Don't give up."

"Stay strong."

I blink rapidly. Right now I don't really feel I'm strong enough but my friends' words of encouragement and hope warm my heart. "Thank you so much, girls."

Nancy clears her throat and clasps her hands in front of that generous décolleté that men go crazy for. "So, Lisa, we're here tonight because we have a little something for you."

I arch my eyebrows. There is a surprise for me? Then maybe this last-minute gathering was not so random, after all.

Nancy finally cuts through my thoughts. "We know the end of your relationship with Nico hit you badly, sweetie, and we want to help. Here," she says, producing an envelope from her glittery purse, "this is from all of us. Each one of us contributed, also Monique, although she couldn't be here tonight."

I look at the girls standing around me: Penny's smirking,

Denise's beaming, and Nancy's grinning. What are they up to?

I take the envelope from Nancy warily "What is this?"

"Just open it and see for yourself," says Nancy, expectantly.

I open the card but it's quite dark in the club. "Is this a list of names?" I ask.

Nancy looks satisfied with my answer. "Smart girl," she says, patting my shoulder gently. "That's exactly what it is: a collection of boyfriend material."

My lips form a perfect 'O' as I skim my eyes over the list. Oh my God, really? I'm not sure how I feel about this list right now. Surprised? Well, yeah, for sure. Confused? I can't deny it; but above all, I'm anxious. Am I really such a hopeless case that my girlfriends think it's necessary to recruit potential boyfriends for me?

"We thought you would want to know who of us was putting each guy forward," Nancy says, beaming. Sure enough, next to each guy's name, there's the name of one of my girlfriends. I shake my head in disbelief. "Well," Nancy says, tapping her long red nail on the first name, "Martin's out already, as we've heard, but Denise insisted that we include him in the card for the record. We thought it'd be fair enough."

Denise tilts her head to the side and shrugs one shoulder.

I close the heart-shaped card. 'Wishing You True Love' I read slowly. I can't believe it: my friends compiled a list of strangers for me to go out on dates with.

Nancy must read the disbelief on my face. "Lisa, sweetie, you are smart, beautiful, and would find a new boyfriend in the blink of an eye if you only wanted to," she says, snapping her fingers. "We just want to encourage you to date and help you find that special someone who will make you happy."

A special someone that will make me happy, I repeat in my head. Until a few months ago, I thought that man was Nico; maybe a part of me still thinks that we'll eventually go back together, but that's just a stupid dream. I shake my head. Maybe it's really time that I move on. I'm not entirely sure that I'm ready to date again right now but the thought that my girlfriends spent time putting together a list of potential candidates for me touches me deeply.

"Thanks so much, girls. Thanks for caring about me and for being so thoughtful. I don't know what to say."

"No problem, sweetie. Just give these guys a chance and see what happens, okay? Who knows, maybe your future husband's name is on that list," Nancy says.

I honestly doubt it, but I bob my head and smile. Then, the practical girl that I am, I can't help but asking about the logistics. "How am I going to get in touch with these guys?" A little hysterical laugh escapes my mouth at the thought of basically cold-calling a bunch of strangers who probably know I'm desperate.

"Ah, you don't need to worry about that, Chica," Penny says, waving a hand. "We'll take care of it." The girls raise their pink and yellow cocktails and cheer to my supposedly bright future full of love.

I take a long gulp and plop down onto the sofa behind me, the soda swashing inside my glass. No need to worry? I think I'm going to pass out.

FOUR

~~Martin Roberts~~ (Denise)
Paco Lopez (Penny)
Jackson Kendall (Nancy)
Paddy Doyle (Monique)
Stephen Adams (Penny)

I'm sitting at my kitchen table, munching on a raisin scone and drinking steaming hot chocolate, but instead of reading the Sunday newspaper, today I'm skimming through my potential boyfriends on the heart-shaped card. The strangers' names look back at me as if they were sets of eyes, but I can't imagine a face framing them. How weird; I haven't even had a drink.

I must confess that I feel a bit intimidated by this 'project,' as Penny calls it. I'm afraid that far too many expectations have been set on the outcome of this social experiment that's more my definition of it and I'm starting to worry that if nothing good comes out of it, my girlfriends will be disappointed.

An image of Denise's contrite face flashes in my mind and I feel guilty all over again. Maybe I should text Martin and apologize. Or maybe I should just dye my hair red, change jobs, or move to Australia, just to reassure my friends that I'm working on my post-break-up drama. Would any of that do?

I look back at the card and realize that Penny put down two names, which somehow adds to the pressure.

"Wow, you referred two guys. There's a lot of people on this short list, isn't there?"

"No, I don't think there is," Penny says nonchalantly, glancing at me over her shoulder. She's chopping potatoes into cubes to make patatas bravas. She loves to cook on Sundays. "Plus, one of those two guys is somebody I know, while the other one is a guy I've never met." Sure enough, there's a little note on the card about the first of her guys, Paco Lopez: *'Brother of my friend Miguel. Never met Paco in person but Miguel says his brother is cool.'* Oh, what a reassuring disclaimer, I mutter, rolling my eyes. I take a sip of my hot chocolate and remind myself that Penny's just trying to help.

"I don't know, Pen," I say warily. "I mean, you are saying you actually don't know this Paco. What's the difference between going out with him or with any stranger I meet in a bar then?"

Penny turns sharply. She looks scary with a long kitchen knife in her hand. Her eyes narrow and I have to remind myself once again that she means well; she always does. "Lisa! You haven't even started the project yet and you're already trying to skip names on the list? No way, missy! You're going out with Paco!"

"I wasn't trying to skip!" I say in a huff, but we both know it's a lie. "Anyway, may I ask how you know Paco's brother at least or is it too much to ask?"

Penny shakes her head and goes back to cutting potatoes. "Paco's brother Miguel and I were in school together in Madrid when we were kids. Now Miguel travels the world. He's a photographer. Paco's his twin."

"And what does Paco do?"

Penny just shrugs my question away and I have the strong feeling that she's not telling me everything she knows about this guy on purpose.

"Penny?"

"I'm not sure what Paco does – a little bit of this, a little bit of that…"

I know my friend well enough to know that she won't tell me more and I just wonder why. For some reason, the idea of going out with this mysterious guy no longer bothers me that much. I guess curiosity is winning over reticence. It's not that I have another option anyway.

"All right, I'll go out with Paco."

"Very good, Chica," Penny says. She throws the little potato cubes into boiling oil and soon enough the fragrance of good, old-school food reaches my nostrils.

My phone vibrates on the kitchen table and I peek at the screen: it's Nico. My heart kicks into overdrive. If I don't take this call, it will be the third one I miss from him this morning.

I should just let the vibration die, but as lame as it is, I want to hear Nico's voice. I don't want Penny to know that I'm talking to my ex again though, she'll give me a hard time if she finds out. She has never truly liked Nico although she has always tolerated him for my sake. Since he dumped me, out of the blue and to sleep around, she's no longer hiding how she feels about him. Nico knows what Penny thinks about him but he doesn't care; he just dismisses every low blow she throws at him with a laugh. That's so typical Nico.

The phone vibrates again. I should really be making an effort to avoid him but the pull is too strong. I snatch up my phone, put my empty mug in the sink as noiselessly as humanly possible, and make a beeline to my room on tiptoe.

"Elisabetta Castelli, you can run and hide in that hole that is your room but I know what you're doing!" Penny yells from the kitchen. I cringe and close the door behind me as I press 'accept call.'

"Hello?"

"Ciao, amore, how are you today?"

I wish Nico's husky voice didn't pour into my ears like one of those captivating melodies you can't get out of your head. I wish his endearment didn't send pleasure waves through all my being but oh, it does. I bask in the feeling of Nico calling me amore, *love*. That's exactly why my phone is glued to my ear right now and I'm experiencing intense guilty pleasure.

I should be angry with my ex for the scene he caused at the pub the other night, but the sad truth is that when Nico goes all caveman with me like that, it turns me on. When he's so possessive, I feel I belong to him, that I belong with somebody, somewhere.

He's not your boyfriend anymore. He has no right.

I square my shoulders. I shouldn't have answered this call so I fake condescension: that's my defense mechanism. "What do you want, Nico?"

He stifles a chuckle. I wish he didn't know me so well. "Why don't you come over here and I'll show you exactly what I want?"

Adrenaline rushes through my veins. I clear my throat.

"How dare you behave as you did, Nico. Why did you have to ruin my night out?"

"That jerk was drunk. You should be more careful. And I think you've lost all your good taste in men since we parted ways. You should do something about that too."

"Like what?" I ask, falling like a rabbit in Nico's rudimental trap. How naïve, I know, but it's too late.

"Just come over here and I'll remind you what you really like." His warm voice is a promise that I know never fails and I'm tempted beyond my best judgment. By the time I hang up on him, I need to double lock myself in my room and hide the key to refrain from running into his open arms. I sigh. I need something to do to distract myself. Yes, I'm going to work for a couple of hours. I take my laptop out from under my bed and boot it.

I go through the notes that my boss, Mr. Conrad, needs typed by noon tomorrow and set to work at a good pace. I'm barely halfway through the second page when my phone beeps and I can't help glancing at the screen. I swear, one of these days I'm going to smash this stupid black rectangle onto the wall!

Nico: Can I come over for lunch?

I bite my lip. Nico loves Spanish food and knows that Penny cooks on Sundays. That's the only reason why he wants to come over here, I tell myself, but I'm secretly thrilled at the prospect of spending some time with him. Maybe we could spend the afternoon together. My pulse accelerates instantly at the possibility of Nico and I alone in my room. I rub my forehead, trying to erase any lustful thoughts from my mind. Nico has this effect on me: he pushes a button deep inside me, one that only he knows where it's hidden, and a river of feel-good hormones get automatically released in my brain. I think I'm addicted to him. *No, you can't do this, Lisa: not any longer,* the little voice in my head reminds me. I inhale deeply and type my answer.

Me: Sorry, I'm not at home

Before I change my mind and text him back, I decide to catch up with my lie and go out for a long walk. I quickly brush my hair, apply my clear lip gloss, and put my flats on. Nancy and her husband John are coming over for lunch anyway today so Penny won't be too disappointed that I won't devour her patatas bravas on the spot, as I always do.

"Penny, please leave some for me for dinner!" I call out, as I rush out of the door.

It's another cold but sunny day, the kind that makes me miss the milder climate of my country. I take a deep breath. After my exchange with Nico earlier, I think some retail therapy is needed so I head to the Camden Markets.

I adore this spot in London. It's crowded and messy, just like my head right now. I gladly get lost in the chaos of colorful stalls and three hours later I'm loaded with bags full of cheap but cute tops and dresses and matching accessories. Among them there's an adorable peach vintage dress dotted with little white flowers that I bought for my date with Paco: it goes well with my blond hair and fair complexion, I think.

As I let myself into my quiet little apartment, my mind drifts back to my confusing situation with Nico. He has made it quite clear that he doesn't want to be committed to me anymore, but he likes to have me when he pleases. That's not enough for me and I told him so, but he still chases me, although I know he can have a different girl every night. He thinks that I'll always be there, holding my breath for him. This is exactly why I'm determined to have a fantastic time with Paco.

In your face, Nico! I say, launching the bags with my newly-acquired belongings in the air. They land disarranged but safely on my bed and I nod to myself with satisfaction.

FIVE

I love my job but sometimes Mr. Conrad gets on my nerves.

I'm not completely sure why but he thinks it's cool to have a foreign personal assistant. Don't take me wrong, I'm obviously glad and thankful for that, and he's a good boss overall. It's just that sometimes, way too close to 6.00pm, he decides that he wants to learn a word or two of Italian. I suspect that's the real reason why he hired me in the first place.

Now I'm all for encouraging the adoption of my native language but with all respect, a donkey would be better at learning languages than poor Mr. Conrad. It takes him like fifteen minutes to memorize a simple sentence that he'll forget by the next day: in other words, he's utterly hopeless at foreign languages, bless him.

I look into Mr. Conrad's thick spectacles and fight the urge to shake my head. Tonight I really don't have time for this: it's my date night with Paco. Earlier this afternoon he texted me the name of the restaurant where we're supposed to meet up and I want to take my time to get ready.

Mr. Conrad finally distorts *ciao bella* one last, painful time and lets me go for the day. I secretly sigh in relief and all but run for the door.

I take the tube – that's how they call the subway in London and hop off at Knightsbridge. Nancy's waiting for me at her salon: she's going to work on me personally tonight. My friend has generously offered to style my hair every time I go out on a date with a new guy on the boyfriend-card, as I've come to call it. This is so kind of her, as there is no way I could afford to have my hair styled as often as I know I will need to over the next weeks. London can be awfully expensive.

"So, who's on tonight?" Nancy asks cheerfully. She's massaging my scalp with her skilled hands and my eyes flutter closed in delight.

"Tonight's guy is Penny's friend's twin brother. His name's Paco."

"Mmmh, Paco… sounds very Latino!"

"Yeah, he's Spanish."

"Are you excited?"

I fidget with the hem of my work shirt. Should I tell Nancy how I actually feel? That I'm anxious as hell about this whole dating thing? On one side I'm still recovering from the disastrous date with Martin, but at the same time I don't want my friend to think that I'm ungrateful. I really appreciate what she and the girls are trying to do for me.

"You don't feel comfortable dating yet, do you, Lisa?" Nancy asks softly, cutting through my thoughts. I shake my shampooed head between her hands. "Give yourself time, sweetie, I promise it will get better," she says, gently tilting my head back.

I close my eyes and warm water falls over my head, washing all the suds away. I wish I was free of my heavy legacy with Nico. I wish I was strong and in control; I wish he didn't tempt me like a ripe, juicy fruit in the middle of a desert, damn him.

"It's just very hard to move on, you know."

"I know. I can see that you still have feelings for Nico. It's tough to walk away from what you know."

"Yeah, it sucks," I say, snorting.

Being open with my friend is liberating and I feel some of the tension leave my shoulders. Nancy's not as judgmental as Penny. Maybe it's just because Penny knows so much more about my tumultuous history with Nico. Living together and being so close, Penny and I can barely hide anything from each other.

"Do you think it's also about that, Nancy? That I'm having a hard time getting over Nico because he's all I know? I don't have any other experience with… men, you know."

"Well, that certainly doesn't help, does it? Despite all the ups and downs, you were comfortable with Nico for a long time. Then, all of a sudden, you found yourself on your own for the first time, and that's pretty disorienting."

I nod. That's exactly how I feel when it comes to my love life: lost and vulnerable. I love that my friend is so perceptive.

Nancy gently towel-dries my hair and wraps my head in a lusciously soft towel. I follow her upstairs and make myself comfortable on a black leather chair in front of a floor-to-ceiling mirror.

"To be honest with you, sweetie, I don't think it's healthy to try as hard as you do to hold on to what you and Nico had," Nancy says, threading a thick comb through my wet locks.

I nod again. Nancy's right: the wisest part of me knows that.

"That's why the girls and I are bullish about you meeting other people, and this is why you're here today. When I'm finished with you, this Paco guy won't know what hit him!"

I smile at Nancy gratefully: confidence injections are always very welcome. My friend works her magic and half an hour later, I'm staring at an improved, glossy-haired version of myself in the huge mirror of Nancy's salon. She's standing right behind me, beaming.

"Have fun tonight, but not too much! Next on the list is my guy, Jackson: believe me, you two are a match made in heaven," she says, winking. I hug her tight and hurry home.

By the time I open the door to my apartment, I've managed to convince myself that instead of using my energy to think about Nico, I should channel it into letting go. What a great attitude to tonight's date: let's see how long it'll last.

I find Penny and Lallo sitting at our kitchen table: Penny is studying, as usual, and Lallo is tampering with the remote. He's been coming around more often lately, helping us with the odd job in the apartment; saying that neither Penny nor I practice DIY successfully is the understatement of the century.

"Hey," I say, walking up to them. "What's up?"

"Hey. Lallo bought us a new remote."

"God bless you, Raffaello," I say dramatically.

"Raffaello?" Penny says, leaning into Lallo. "Is that your real name?"

"Yeah."

"What?" I ask innocently. "It's a lovely name."

Lallo's expression shifts to one I can't read then he clears his voice. "So, big date tonight, uh?" he asks casually, casting his glance back down at the remote.

His question takes me off guard but I keep my face straight. Lallo and I are childhood friends and it's true that we watch out for each other, but why would he ask about my date? Did Penny tell him about Paco? Unless... wait a minute, I think I know what's going on here: Lallo must be spying on me on Nico's behalf. Well, to be completely honest, I'm dreading this date, but by God, Nico is never going to find out. I certainly don't want my ex to think that I'm sitting at home alone and in despair just because he ditched me for free loving. That thought is so frustrating that it makes me want to grab the two coffee cups sitting on the table and smash them against the wall.

"It's going to be a great night, I can't wait!" I answer, way too brightly. Penny snorts: I'm so going to strangle her later. Lallo looks between the two of us and it's my cue to go get ready before my glare reduces my smartass roommate to ashes.

"Just... be careful, okay?" Lallo says. That makes me pause on my foot: whatever his motives for asking me about tonight, I know that Lallo cares about me. He's a wonderful friend.

"I will, Daddy," I say, smiling over my shoulder, sincerely this time.

I take a quick shower, slide into my new dress and heels, and carefully apply my makeup. I check the time. It looks like I made it, after all; I'm ready five minutes before my cab arrives. I'm wearing super high heels and I have no intention of ruining my feet by walking unnecessarily.

I'm meeting Paco at La Cave, a trendy French restaurant in Mayfair. Like most Italians, I love good food and right now I'm starving. As soon as I enter the restaurant, I realize that I have no clue what my date looks like. I groan at my stupidity. How haven't I thought about this? It's not like the guy's going to show up with a red rose between his teeth, is he? I guess I'm officially incompetent at blind dating.

I scan the copper and white-themed bar at the front of the restaurant. Maybe Paco is the rangy guy sipping a cocktail on a stool on the corner. He looks cute. Nah, for some reason I don't think that's him. As if on cue, a girl walks up to the guy and kisses him on the lips. Well, I just hope that's not my date!

I feel a light tap on my shoulder. I turn around and my eyes meet with dark, intense ones: for a moment I'm taken aback.

"Are you Lisa?" the guy asks with a strong Spanish accent.

I nod silently, my gears spinning: I've seen this guy before. He looks familiar but I can't place his face right now. All I know is that he's jaw-dropping beautiful: there's no way I could forget his face. I quickly browse through friends' and acquaintances' faces in my head but I can't come up with anything.

Paco smirks at my obvious confusion and it finally hits me: this guy's face is all over London! If I'm not wrong, he's the testimonial of a mobile provider's campaign. Oh God, I'm so out of my league here that I want to scream at the top of my lungs right now. I silently curse Penny in my native language for setting me up with this impossibly hot stranger, and believe me, nothing compares to Italian when it comes to swearing.

Paco arches an eyebrow and tilts his head to the side. I guess I'm staring.

"Hi," I say a little breathlessly. Am I really going to have dinner with Paco Lopez, as in the Paco-Lopez-the-model? But, more surprisingly, why on earth is he going to have dinner with a 'nobody' like me? He surely mingles with famous actresses and other heavenly females. How did you manage to pull this trick, Penny? I ask my roommate mentally. An image of her weird candles flashes my mind and I suddenly feel a renewed respect for Penny's witchcraft abilities. I think I underestimated my roommate, by far.

Paco shakes my hand firmly. "Nice to meet you, Lisa. Shall we go find our table?" he asks, amused. He must know his looks have the 'wow' factor and he obviously enjoys every second of arousing the kind of reaction I've just had when my jaw dropped and I had to collect it from the tiled floor. I just wished he had introduced himself, instead of assuming I had recognized him. I mean, I get that he's famous and all, but isn't that a bit cocky of him? Nico would always introduce himself to his fans, even to those who clearly knew who he was, because they had paid a considerable amount of money to watch The Lost Souls perform at exclusive venues.

We follow a waiter through the restaurant. The place is decorated in copper and white with big mirrors on the walls, just like the bar, but I barely notice. I'm too busy blushing, staring at this Spaniard's fine butt and wondering again why on earth Paco Lopez would agree to waste his time with me. For sure Penny must have claimed a huge favor from her former classmate Miguel; there's no other explanation.

Glances shoot in Paco's direction from every corner of the room. His looks are truly exceptional. Well, I may be mourning the end of my relationship with Nico, but I'm not dead. He walks with measured, confident strides, his proportioned body moving with a lazy elegance. The women seem particularly smitten with him and I don't blame them, nor am I surprised. It's like with Nico: he turns heads. Nico's face is not only very attractive, though, it's mesmerizing in an imperfect sort of way. Stop thinking about Nico, you fool! I chastise myself as we finally reach our destination after Paco's little catwalk.

Our table is at the back of the restaurant, in a corner; for privacy, I suppose. We sit down and I immediately skim through the menu to avoid Paco's assessing gaze and any unwanted thoughts of my ex. Tonight it's about me and I'm starving.

A smiling waitress shows up at our table and I start giving her my order. I love French food and I know what I want.

"May I have the pâté d'Ardennes as a starter, the baked goat's cheese salad with Honey and Walnut oil dressing, the confit of duck with Port wine sauce, oh, and a side of potato croquettes, please," I say, without missing a beat. I close the menu and raise my eyes. Paco is staring at me and he looks horrified.

I press my hand to my chest self-consciously. What did I do?

"Madre de Dios," Paco barks. "You are slim, girl, but you eat like a pig!"

My jaw drops in shock. What the hell?! "I beg your pardon?"

Paco leans forward. "Are you sure you wanna eat all that

food, gorgeous? What you've just ordered is probably over one thousand nine hundred calories, which is pretty much the entire daily calories intake recommended for women."

I blink quickly, forcing my breath out through my nose. Who is this guy, the Rain Man of bloody calories? My instinct screams to get the hell out of here and put as much distance as possible between my healthy self and this rude paranoiac, but I just sit there, frozen: I already dread the debriefing of my date with Penny.

If I run away from this guy like I did with Martin, my friends will think that I'm a lunatic. To add to the awkwardness of the moment, my stomach decides to rumble loudly. Great job, Lisa!

I make up my mind and square my shoulders: since I'm in a fancy French restaurant and I'm hungry, I'll just eat my dinner and try to have a good time, despite the very good-looking but unfortunately idiotic company.

By now the waitress is shifting uncomfortably from one foot to the other.

"How about we share what I've just ordered?" I offer in a way too- pitched voice.

Paco scratches his strong chin. "All right, but you have the croquettes, and I'll have the salad. I don't eat fried stuff." Figures. I smile apologetically at the waitress. We won't be ordering wine, I guess. She runs away from our table as if a ball of fire was chasing her.

I spend the rest of the evening making small talk with a self-absorbed, food-phobic, male model. Who'd have thought that this popular, astonishing- looking guy would be so lame? When he starts to talk about his adventures at the latest Paris fashion week, my bored mind drifts to its favorite subject: Nico.

My ex can also be a jerk at times, but sure enough he's not nearly as conceited as Paco. Nico is a fantastic songwriter, singer and guitarist; but humble, nonetheless. And let's be honest: looks-wise, Nico is as good as Paco, just coarser, kind of rougher around the edges... Stop it, Lisa! I kick myself mentally for my little clandestine escape and make a point of spending the rest of the evening now and here with Paco, trying to focus on every futile word he says.

He finally walks me out of the restaurant, putting an end to this torture.

Despite our obvious incompatibility, for some reason, Paco is not ready to let me go. My guess is that this is very much about his male pride, or maybe just lust; it's probably about both.

He takes my hand and traces slow circles on my skin with his thumb. "You're not my type, mi amor, but I like you. I'm flying out to Los Angeles tomorrow but I wouldn't mind sleeping with you tonight; that is, if you have nothing better to do," he says smugly, as if to challenge me to contradict him.

Oh, but I do have something better to do, Paco: I can't get home fast enough to make myself a toast, because you ate half of my food tonight, I accuse him mentally.

"Thank you for... offering, I guess... but I don't do one-night stands." I'm quite happy with my answer: it's neutral, I hope, but at the same time it's as good as saying that I will never sleep with him, which makes sense, since I'm pretty sure I won't see Paco ever again.

He scratches his chin and gives me his first, truly genuine smile tonight. I must admit that he is charming when he takes off the celebrity hat. "No," he says chuckling, "you're definitely not my type."

Ten minutes later, I'm riding home in a cab half asleep when my phone beeps, startling me. I fish it out of my bag.

Nico: I'm all alone in my bed. I miss you. Do u wanna come over?

A rush of adrenaline pumps through my veins instantly and in the blink of an eye, I'm fully alert.

When Nico texts me in the middle of the night, I'm usually sound asleep but tonight my dinner with Paco left me empty, in every way. The truth is that I feel lonelier than ever.

If temptation was a sin, you would be burning in hell, I tell myself. I read Nico's text again and again and quickly consider my options, but my mind is already made up, damn him. That's right: I guess it didn't take much to persuade me.

I give Nico's address to the taxi driver. It does bother me

that it's so easy for him to pull me to him whenever he wants but I really need him badly tonight.

Me: Who do you think you are?

I fidget with the hem of my dress until my phone finally beeps again.

Nico: The door is unlocked. Come soon

I pay the cabby and quickly hop out of the car. Nico's street is in a residential area and it's deserted at this time of the night. Butterflies dance in my stomach as I take the stairs two at a time, risking my neck in my high heels: yes, I'm beyond dignity, and the worse thing is that at this moment in time, I don't care. There's a superior force propelling me up these stairs and towards my ex-boyfriend's arms right now, and I don't care about anything else in the world. How ironic that the source of this powerful energy is actually my own weakness.

I take a few steadying breaths and knock softly at Nico's door. It flings open and closed and before I can blink, my back is pushed against hard wood and Nico's hungry mouth closes over mine. I open to him, his tongue warm and delicious in my mouth, and we take and give with equal eagerness.

"Why did it take you so long?" he whispers in Italian, against my swollen lips. He is flush against me and his hands are sliding over the sides of my tights, slowly lifting my dress.

"Why would you think I'd run to you?"

Nico's mouth curves in what has become his signature smirk and I instantly melt right at his feet. I'd do anything to make this bad boy smile.

"Come," he commands, taking a step back. He tugs me to his bedroom and my racing heart skips a beat in anticipation. I walk into his room and inhale deeply. This is my favorite place in his apartment: Nico's clean, masculine scent permeates the air.

His burning eyes skim up and down my body appreciatively. "You look beautiful tonight. It used to take you ages to get all dolled up," he says, walking me backwards to his bed

I snort. "I bet you think this is for you?" I ask, skimming

my hand over my fancy hairdo, down the length of my pale neck, over my breasts, my hip, down to the hem of my sexy peach dress. "What makes you think this is for you?"

Nico's eyes narrow only for a fraction of a second and I smile triumphantly as I catch a glimpse of his annoyance, before it dissolves.

"Well, you're here, aren't you?" he says, shrugging one shoulder.

And here I am indeed, basking in every sensation I can like a starved woman. One by one, with excruciating slowness, Nico removes all the hairpins from my blond tresses until they cascade wildly down my bare shoulders. He buries his fingers in my hair and clenches his fist at the base of my nape, tugging gently, exposing my neck to his sensual assault. Oh God. A shiver explodes between my shoulder blades and all I can think about is that I want every inch of my ex-boyfriend tonight.

My hands fist in Nico's dark curls and he devours my neck, knocking the breath out of me. He inhales deeply into my hair and bites my earlobe, licking his mark with his soft, warm tongue. Tingles course over me from head to toe and my eyes flutter closed in delight.

"Are you gonna tell me who you wore this little number for?"

I open my eyes reluctantly and push forward to meet his pout with my hungry lips but he holds me back, keeping me inches away from what I crave most. I tilt my chin down and look up at him through my black thick lashes. "For nobody," I murmur, biting my lower lip.

Nico stares at my mouth for a long moment then he shakes his head. "You are going to kill me, Elisabetta," he drawls, and I fall back onto his big bed, taking him down with me.

I love the feeling of Nico on me. He's tall and built, smooth and hard; he's gorgeous. His sculpted lips are hovering just inches over mine and his warm, minty breath fans my face deliciously while he searches my eyes.

"Kiss me," he orders. I slowly shake my head. "Kiss me," he says again, more gently. I push my head up to meet his lips but he pulls away. I narrow my eyes. He knows I hate it when he does that. I push against his weight but he's too heavy to shove away; he just adjusts his strong body against mine in an angle that makes me shiver with desire. He traces my parted lips with his tongue and this time he doesn't pull away when I capture his smirk in my mouth.

***

One hour later, Nico is skimming his hand lazily over my body. "Are you sure you don't want to sleep here tonight?"

"I can't," I say, shoving his hand off my bare belly and sliding out of his bed. Coming here was a bad, bad idea I already regret.

He chuckles softly and arranges his pillow more comfortably under his head as he watches me dress. "As you wish, amore mio."

"I'm not your love, Nico," I hiss, sliding back into my dress. "Wouldn't you know? You don't want to be with me."

Nico moans into the pillow and rolls onto his back, draping an arm over his eyes. I lick my lips instinctively. It's not my fault if he's a vision, with only a white sheet barely covering his hot body… I need to get out of here before my resolve to leave dissolves. "Elisabetta, you know I care about you. I always will."

I know, and he knows that's not enough for me, but I'm exhausted and it's too late to start a fight. "Goodnight, Nico."

"Night, amore," he says, air-kissing me from the bed. Jerk. I shut the door behind me loudly.

Thank God there are plenty of cabs in London and they work at all hours. I don't have the strength to walk the short distance to my apartment. I hail a taxi and step in. I push the key into my apartment's lock extra carefully. The last thing I need now is to wake Penny up and be grilled about my date with Paco. That surely can wait until tomorrow morning.

I open the door warily and I'm surprised to find the lamp on in the living room. Penny is snoozing softly, snuggled on one side of our green old couch. Lallo is sitting on the other side of the couch, scribbling on a notebook. He looks up when he sees me. Black circles under his eyes make him look very tired; it's a week day and it's very late. What is he doing still here?

"Hey," I whisper, waving my hand.

"Hey, did you have a good night?" Lallo asks, taking me in.

I thread my fingers through my tousled hair self-consciously, hoping that the dim light of the lamp will cover the heat of my cheeks. I feel like my dad caught me sneaking back home after I partied wildly all night long.

"It was good enough," I say nonchalantly. "Have you been composing?" I ask him, desperate for a change of subject. This is so embarrassing.

"Yeah, I was just putting down a few words. Well," he says, closing his notepad and pushing himself up from the couch, "at least you're back in one piece."

I smile at Lallo: it's so sweet of my friend to worry about me.

"Good night, Lisa, sleep well," he says, walking around me towards the door.

"You too. Thanks for making sure that I'm safe home."

"Anytime. You know you can always count on me," Lallo says over his shoulder, closing the door behind him.

SIX

"Why didn't you wake me up? My neck hurts!" Penny moans, rubbing her nape as I pour a cup of coffee for her. I've already drunk mine, I have an early start today.

They say that every cloud has a silver lining: well, since I've been single, I've had more time for myself; that's one of the few positive things of my forced status. On Mondays, Wednesdays, and Fridays, I go for a run in Hyde Park before work. Running frees my mind and helps me keep fit. I was hoping that today Penny would oversleep until I'd be back from my run, as she'd usually do, but I was fooling myself. The twinkle in her eyes tells me that she can't wait to know about my date with Paco. I put the steaming coffee cup down in front of her and thread my fingers through my hair to fix it in a ponytail.

"You looked so snuggly on the couch with Lallo last night that I didn't want to wake you up," I say, smiling sweetly.

Penny glares at me. "We were just waiting for you to be back."

"Oh yeah, of course you were 'waiting for me' sleeping like a log!"

"Whatever," Penny says, waving a hand and taking a sip of her coffee. "Anyway, how did your date go? Tell, tell, tell!"

"Hey, that's my scone for later!" I protest.

"Sharing is caring, Chica," she says innocently, biting on my breakfast.

"Well, speaking about *sharing*, I would have appreciated if you'd told me that I was going to have dinner with a model!" My eyes narrow on Penny's smug expression behind the rim of her cup.

"You knew, didn't you? You knew who Paco was and you didn't tell me! 'What does he do?' - 'A little bit of this, a little bit of that'... What were you thinking, Penny?"

She holds up her hands in defense. "Hey, I suspected that he was famous, but I wasn't sure!"

"Ha! As if I believe you now!" I say, lifting my feet on the chair in front of me and tying my laces.

"What's the problem anyway?" Penny asks, looking up at me.

"Oh, nothing, you know. I was just wondering what Miguel exactly owed you to send his famous brother out on a date with an ordinary girl like me?"

Penny's lips curve in a knowing smile and I know that she's not going to tell me about her past with Miguel. But she sobers up quickly. "Don't talk about yourself like that. I don't like it. You're no ordinary person. You're very special. Did you have a good time with Paco?"

I ponder how much of my disappointment I should share with Penny, and opt for a light version of how I feel. "He's a great guy but I don't think there's ever going to be a second date, unfortunately," I say, carefully.

"Why?"

I roll my eyes. Leave it to Penny to be subtle. "He's gorgeous, but we didn't really click and I don't think we share the same values, you know."

"I see," Penny says. She watches me carefully while I slide into my fleece and zip it up, and I swear I can see the gears in her head go into overdrive. "What time did you come home last night? You weren't at home when I last checked."

"Penny, will you please stop interrogating me? It's annoying. This is our kitchen plates, cutlery, cooking pans everywhere. See? We're not in court and I'm not accused of murder or anything else," I blabber, waving my hands nervously.

Penny shakes her head. "I just hope it's not as I think."

A sense of uneasiness sets on my shoulders and I cringe. I feel like a user who's desperately trying to hide her addiction. When did Nico become my drug? That must have happened long ago, but we were a couple back then and as such I had free access to him, so I didn't realize how dependent I'd become... I suddenly need to get out of my apartment, quickly. I start to jog in place, my blond ponytail swinging behind my head. "I'm running late, Pen, see you tonight," I say, as I run for the door.

"Just remember to strikethrough Paco's name on the card!" Penny calls out from the kitchen.

***

I put away the last of the files I've worked on this morning. I've been assisting Mr. Conrad with a confidential reorganization that is going to happen in a few weeks.

My boss has been quite secretive about this deal and that's unusual of him. Under normal circumstances he would share more details with me, but not this time, and I've been wondering if my job is at risk. I really hope that giving me the boot is not a part of this top-priority plan he's been working on. Maybe I should start looking around for a new job, but I'm reluctant to. Despite the crisis, GBG Insurance is a fast-growing company and despite his stubbornness with learning Italian, I genuinely like working for Mr. Conrad.

I check the time and grab my jacket. I'm having lunch with Monique. I haven't seen her in a while and I can't wait to hear why she couldn't go with me and the girls to Yoyo. I just hope she and Andy haven't broken up, they are a wonderful couple.

I step out of the GBG building. It's cold and pouring rain outside. You gotta love spring in London, I mutter. I hold my red umbrella firmly above my head and walk the short distance to Dino's in record time.

The little restaurant is packed, as it always is at this time, but I reserved a table. Monique is not here yet so I sit down at a small table. Scrolling through my messages, I read Nico's text again and smile. His birthday is just a few days away. The only one of his birthday parties that I missed was when I was nine and I went down with chicken pox. The next day Nico had come to visit me and brought me a slice of cake he'd saved for me. Deep down, Nico's always been a sweetheart: it's just recently that he has turned into a selfish jerk. Maybe I wasn't such a bad influence when I was his girlfriend after all.

On my way to work this morning, I called Lallo to fish for more information about Nico's birthday party: apparently it's a big deal for Nico and he's determined to make a memorable event of it. I just hope there won't be too many girls. My stomach contracts at the thought of Nico with another woman. I take a deep breath to ease my sudden discomfort: Nico being promiscuous is one of the things about us no longer being together that I still can't digest.

I'm indulging in sad, jealousy-provoked thoughts when I hear my name: Monique is walking up to me, wrapped in a cream wool cardigan that looks as soft as it feels when I stand up and wrap her in a tight hug. She hugs me back and I gasp in surprise. "Oh my God, Monique!" I shriek, looking down at her hint of a baby bump.

"I know, I know! It just didn't feel right to tell you on the phone and we could never arrange to meet up!" she says, giggling. It's at that very moment that I get it, what they mean when they say that expecting women have a glow about them. My friend is radiant, she looks incredible. I shake my head in wonder and just mirror her infectious beam.

We sit down and the waiter comes over immediately. "A Caesar salad and still water for you, right?" he asks, taking the menu from me, and I nod. "Have you decided, Monique, or do you need more time?"

Monique places her order then she sits back in her chair and smiles knowingly. "You must be kidding me. How did the waiter know what you wanted before you ordered?"

"I come here often," I say defensively, but it sounds lame even to my own ears.

"Always adventurous, aren't you, Lisa?" Monique asks, amused.

"I know, I'm quite predictable, I guess," I mumble. Maybe I'm just boring. Maybe that's why Nico left me in the first place. *Stop battering yourself down, Lisa!* Seriously, I think I need to start listening to the little voice in my head.

"Ah honey, there's nothing wrong with that, as long as you try new things, or men, every once in a while," Monique says, winking, and I can't help but laugh with her.

"By the way, thanks for the card, I guess."

"You're very welcome. I hope we didn't offend you. We really just want to help. Nico has done enough damage and you've wasted enough time."

"Mmm hmm." As you may have figured out, Monique doesn't like Nico very much.

"Paddy, my guy, is fantastic. There's something about Irish men, trust me!" my friend says. That doesn't surprise me: her boyfriend Andy is a Dubliner.

We chat away while we wait for our food and drinks. Monique tells me about her pregnancy, how she found out, what Andy said, what names they like. She's happy. I just sit there and do my best to absorb her positive energy. I feel like I'm having lunch with the sun on this miserable rainy day.

The waiter brings our orders and while she digs into her spaghetti, I take a moment to observe my friend from behind the rim of my glass. Monique is a mum-to-be and that puts everything into prospective. My obsessive thinking about Nico's birthday party seems so trivial now that I want to hide under the table in shame. Actually, I think it's more than that. Monique is so sure about what she wants out of her future; after all, she's literally *creating* her future inside of herself right now. On the other hand, my life is rickety. I'm unfocused and I don't know what I really want, or maybe I do know more than I want to admit.

I know that I want a man like Andy in my life, or like John, Nancy's husband; someone who loves me and is securely by my side. I want somebody loyal, caring, who wants a family; but then again, I don't seem able to see past Nico and the fact that 'ex' and 'forever' don't belong together in the same sentence. Another thing I know is that this on-and-off thing with Nico is consuming me. I've never been more sure that it's bad for me than at this very moment that I'm looking into my friend's deep black eyes.

After a delightful lunch, I hug Monique goodbye, careful not to squash her belly, and head back to the office. The rain has stopped and a few rays of sunshine are filtering through the clouds. As I expertly hop on my high heels to skip a bigger puddle, I admit to myself that despite everything, I really want to go to Nico's birthday party. But how am I going to get this past Penny I wonder; I doubt she'll take it well.

The afternoon flies between meetings, bouncing calls that Mr. Conrad has no time to take, and working on making the annual company's summer party happen. I love organizing fun events and today I welcome this break from self-commiseration more than ever.

Some people consider corporate events an obligation, but I think it's very generous of Mr. Conrad to offer his employees a summer party on top of the Christmas party we have every year. I'm thrilled that my boss entrusted me to organize the summer party this year. I'll work on it with Sarah, a girl who's just back from maternity leave. I've met her couple of times before and she seems nice. I care a lot about this event: I'm going to make good use of the budget Mr. Conrad allocated for this party and make sure everybody has a good time.

"This is going to be fun," Sarah says sarcastically, skimming through the first draft of the guest list. "Are these all employees? I don't recognize some of the names."

"The majority are employees; some of them were probably hired while you were on leave. The others are external partners and consultants that Mr. Conrad wants to extend the invite to."

"I see," she says in a clipped voice.

I think that being recently back from maternity leave is taking its toll on Sarah. I wish I could ease her tension. "It's going to be fine, you'll see. We have plenty of time to organize this event."

"Yeah, you're right. I guess I just feel a bit overwhelmed. I've never tried to please three hundred people at once," she says, snorting

I look up from my laptop: Sarah is frowning. I feel like her concern is more about her needing to adjust to being back to work than the actual challenge of putting together this party. I decide that she'll have my full support, woman to woman.

"Well, Sarah, if you put it like that, no wonder you're worried! You'll see, we're gonna find amazing attractions never seen before to entertain our guests. I promise you they will never forget this party."

"Attractions? Like what?" she asks, alarmed.

"An alien? Popcorn dispensers? Elephants?"

Sarah bites back a chuckle and goes back to her list. "We'll need music," she says, looking above my head and I mentally praise her. She's already switched to positive, productive mood.

"Great point. What's a party without music?"

"My husband is a sound engineer. He works in a recording studio. I could ask him if anybody's interested in playing at our party and how much it would cost."

"That would be fantastic! I'll put your name next to this task then," I say, winking. Under other circumstances I would have asked my boyfriend's band to play, but that is never going to happen now and I'm actually grateful that Sarah has offered to take care of that bit.

My phone beeps in my hand just as I'm leaving for the day. Tonight I'm supposed to meet with Jackson, Nancy's guy, for the first time, but it looks like that won't be the case.

Hi, it's Jackson. I was delayed in a meeting and I missed my flight. I'll text you to reschedule when I'm back in London. Sorry for the short notice.

'I'll text you to reschedule'? What does this guy think I am, one of his work incumbencies? I shrug my shoulders. I don't really care. Is it very bad that I feel relieved that Jackson is not in London? The truth is that I'm still getting over the Paco shock and the last thing I feel like doing tonight is going out with another stranger. I call Nancy to cancel my first-date hair appointment and head straight home, scanning my head to remember if tonight is movie night on Channel 2. Dear old couch, here I come!

I close my apartment door behind me and I find Penny grumbling in Spanish, curling her long black hair in front of the living room mirror, or at least trying to do just that. "Here, let me do it," I say, shrugging out of my jacket and taking the curler from her.

Penny scowls at me. "I hate this stupid curler. It's taking me forever!"

"Hey, I'm here to help!"

She huffs and I bite back a smile. Penny hates 'trivial tasks,' as she calls them, such as styling her hair; and she's jealous of my naturally wavy hair. Hers is bone-straight.

"Hot date tonight?"

"Nah," she says. "Do you remember Danny? He's doing the master's with me."

"Danny-the-cute-guy-who-has-it-bad-for-you?"

Penny rolls her eyes. "Danny's cousin David is visiting from Bristol. We're just going out for a beer. By the way, what are doing home so early? Shouldn't you be with Nancy right now?"

Penny eyes me suspiciously in the mirror in front of us. I know she thinks that I'm skipping tonight's date and I take a big, calming breath. "It's not like you think, Penny. Nancy's guy cancelled, or I should say, 'he postponed and will text me back to reschedule,' to quote his own words."

Penny narrows her eyes. "He postponed."

It's my turn to glare. I can't believe she's probing!

"Apparently, he's stuck somewhere for business, but who knows," I say, rolling another one of Penny's thick tresses around the hot curler. "I mean, maybe he's not completely comfortable with this dating thing and he's chickening out."

"Maybe," Penny concedes.

"So who's this cousin of Danny's?" I've heard Penny talk about her classmate but never about his cousin before.

"I don't know actually, I've never met him. Hey, why don't you come out with us tonight and find out for yourself?"

Oh, no, please. No. "Thanks, but I think I'll play good housewife. I have a mountain of laundry and ironing to do." What I really want to do is curl up on our old green couch with a greasy chocolate bar and catch up on my favorite series. I cross my fingers and hope Penny will let this go, but I should know better.

"Come on, Lisa, it's just for a couple of hours. If Jackson hadn't cancelled last minute, you'd have gone out anyway, wouldn't you?"

Penny has a point, of course. Well, she always does: she's a law student and a practitioner.

"I'd rather stay at home tonight," I plead.

Penny pins me with her severe gaze and shakes her head and I know I don't stand a chance. She'll bug me until I agree to go out with them.

I finish doing Penny's hair and jump in the shower. This better be a fun night, I say to myself as I thread my fingers through my damp hair. Half an hour later, Penny and I are both dressed and ready to go.

We meet the guys in the busy West End. Danny wants to show David the club where he works in the weekends. The place doesn't look special from the outside but as we step in, I realize that the inside is really something. The walls are all black and plastered with posters, pictures, fliers and bands' framed autographs. I instantly like this place: it's packed with people chatting loudly and obviously having a good time.

Danny leads us to the bar, where he shakes hands and exchanges a few words with the bartender in charge tonight.

"I like your jeans, they suit you," David says.

I skim my hands over my red skinny jeans self-consciously. I just hope Danny's cousin won't hit on me: there's only so much a girl can take. "Thanks."

"What will you have?" he asks. His blond bangs keep falling in his eyes, no matter how often he pushes them back.

"A Coke, please."

He arches his eyebrows. "A Coke?"

"I don't drink." You see, that's why I don't particularly like going to bars or clubs with people I don't know because then I have to explain that no, I don't drink, and no, I'm not allergic to alcohol, and no, I'm not ten years old. "I just don't like drinking, that's all."

David looks at me as if I've grown a second head and I go back to scanning the wall behind the bar. The number of famous bands that have played in this place over the years is remarkable.

"You work in a very cool place," I tell Danny when he turns to us. He rewards me with a huge grin. He looks quite cute in that grey shirt he's sporting tonight. I wonder if Penny has noticed too, but I have a feeling her thoughts are on somebody else. She has been acting strangely lately, ending phone calls abruptly when I walk into the room.

We follow Danny to a table with a 'reserved' tag on it. We sit down just when a band is coming out on stage. I look down at the flier that the girl at the entrance pushed in my hand. These must be the InTouch, the supporting band to the main act.

"Danny, what's the main band playing tonight? Why's the name not on the flier?" I ask.

"Only supporting bands are showing in this club's fliers: it's to let emerging bands be in the spotlight for once and to surprise the audience. Don't worry, though, all the main acts that perform in here are super cool."

Oh. My excitement kicks in, triggering my internal alarm.

One-two, one-two. The InTouch front man checks the mike and shortly afterwards the band kick off their performance with a powerful song that sets the mood for the next three they play. I watch them doing their thing while I sip at my drink, getting more and more nervous by the minute. I glance Penny's way a few times but she's engrossed in a conversation with David, while Danny's tapping his fingers on the table at the fast rhythm of the music.

InTouch play their last song and leave the stage to the sound of loud clapping. I guess they did well, but I couldn't say: I haven't really been paying attention. All I've been thinking about is when these teenagers would finally be finished so I could see who would be playing next.

"I bet you know who's playing tonight," David says, nudging his cousin.

"Ouch! Of course I do!"

"Are you gonna tell us or what?" Penny asks, sternly. Let's just say that she's not the most patient person in the world.

I take a sip of my Coke and almost spit it out when I see Nico, Lallo, Jude, and Bruce walk on stage. The clapping and cheering of the audience is deafening now. I'm proud of Nico. He's come a long, long way since he strummed away in my parents' backyard on his first little guitar covered in football player stickers.

I haven't seen Nico since we spent our last night together.

His magnificent presence on stage makes my pulse race. I've missed him. I glance at Penny guiltily. I actually expect her to make up an excuse to leave right now but she's just staring at the stage, transfixed. I know she likes the band but her reaction throws me off. She must feel my eyes on her because she looks back at me and mouths "Are you alright?" Obviously, I'm not: I'm hot and bothered and my heart is jumping out of my chest, but I shrug as nonchalantly as I can. Penny focuses back on the stage and, just like that, we can stay.

I exhale in relief and let my eyes drift back to Nico. I don't think he can see me but oh, boy, can I see him. He's sporting a green t-shirt; people wouldn't be able to tell in this dim light but it matches the color of his eyes. Nico's black hair is styled in a just-out-of-bed mess and his pout is right in place. He's always worn his bad boy mask whenever he performs; the problem is that now he never seems to take it off, even off stage. Sitting on a stool, skimming his long fingers over his shiny black guitar, he looks good enough to eat and all I want to do right now is jump on that stage and drag him home with me.

Apparently, I'm not the only one who wouldn't mind doing just that. There's a table in turmoil in front of the stage: a group of girls is talking excitedly. They giggle, look at Nico, and then giggle again. One of them, a brunette with legs that go on forever, is particularly animated. Every time she jumps and waves, her extra-large boobs bounce happily. Nico doesn't seem to notice: he's engrossed in tuning his guitar. I fight the instinct to strangle the parade of bimbos, the brunette first of all, and be done with their enthusiasm. I swallow down my jealousy and clench my big cold glass with ten fingers.

Nico's mellow voice addresses the audience with just a touch of accent that is so familiar to me, and that is enough to make me purr in my chair. The Lost Souls start to play one of their masterpieces and the club goes wild. A shiver runs up my spine at the memory of where Nico composed the lyrics of this fast-paced love ballad one fine summer afternoon: on my bare back, as I lay sprawled on a blanket on the bank of Lake Como. *Come to me, set me free*, Nico sings invitingly, and my blood rushes in my veins. No matter how many times I've seen him on stage, I always get a kick from watching Nicolas Neri own his scene.

When Nico's up there on stage, he's wild and sexy as hell, just like he is under the sheets. My cheeks burn and I chastise myself mentally for going there, but what can I do? That place, where I can indulge in lustful fantasies about Nico, seems to be my favorite spot lately. If you can't find me, well, I'm probably there. I shift my gaze to the back of the stage. Lallo is punishing the drums like there's no tomorrow and I catch Penny watching him.

Ah-ha! I've been suspecting that Penny has an interest in Lallo but now I know for sure. It's written all over her face. An idea forms in my mind: maybe Lallo is my pass to Nico's birthday party.

"Penny!" I call over the music. She leans forward, removing her gaze from Lallo reluctantly. "Nico invited us to his birthday party. There's gonna be a lot of people, like, you know, his band mates and others. Shall we go?" I know, I can be sneaky sometimes.

"I don't know," Penny says. "Are you sure it's a good idea? Will you be okay?"

I look straight into her eyes and I see it there: expectation. Penny wants me to say that I'll be okay and we should go. I can feel it; so, the good friend that I am, I oblige. I lean back on my chair, smirking to myself. This was way easier than I thought. I take a sip of my Coke and go back to eye-eating my breath-taking ex as he pours his soul into the mike.

"Shall we go, girls?" Danny says after a couple of songs. "Penny and I have class tomorrow and David's flying out at 7.00am."

We stand up to leave. I catch Nico flashing a rare smile at the busty brunette at the front table and my fists clench at my sides. Now that I look at her closer, I actually think I've seen this girl before. She must be one of the hard-core groupies who won't miss any of the band's concerts for anything in the world. I bet she can't wait to sleep with one of the guys and I'll take a guess about who her first choice might be. Argh! Am I pushing my imagination too far? Maybe, but now I wish I could stay till the end of the concert to see if Nico will leave with this girl. Actually, I know that's what he'll do. That's why he left me, after all, to sleep around with 34D groupies. My heart beats like crazy as I follow Penny and the guys to the door, forcing one heavy foot in front of the other.

***

I lie in my bed, unable to sleep. The thought of Nico taking another woman back to his place is killing me. I slap my pillow in frustration and readjust it under my head.

My phone lights up in the dark by my bed and I fight the urge to snatch it up. Don't look, I tell myself, but curiosity quickly has the better of my shaky will.

Nico: I saw you tonight. Red suits you.

Oh! I turn on my night lamp. I hadn't realized that Nico had seen me at the club. I glance knowingly at the red jeans I dropped on the chair by my desk earlier.

Nico: Who were the two losers you girls were with?

My excitement quickly turns into irritation. Why does Nico always have to question who I spend my time with, while I have no insight or say whatsoever in who he mingles, or sleeps, with? He wants to be with other women, that's why he left me, so how dare he judge Penny's friends?

I turn onto my stomach and type my angry reply.

Why do you care who I was with?

I wait, boiling slowly in my annoyance, but Nico's not answering and it's not long before self-doubt creeps on me. Maybe I was too harsh: he just tried to ask about my life and I put him off with a rude text. He had just complimented me. Maybe he went home alone; he's texting me, after all. Maybe he still cares about me and he's just jealous.

I stare at my phone's dark screen, getting more anxious by the minute. Did Nico fall asleep? It's two in the morning, after all. I'm exhausted, I should try to sleep too but I'm restless and if I don't talk to Nico right now, I won't be able to sleep a wink.

I know I shouldn't do it but I quick-dial Nico's number: he's still my number one, even in my phone settings. I tap my feet nervously on the mattress. The line rings once, twice, three times. *You shouldn't have called, Lisa.* I bury my head in my hand: I hate it when my inner voice states the obvious. Maybe he did fall asleep after all. I'm just about to press 'end call' when Nico picks up.

"Hey," he whispers. His voice is warm and raspy and I jump off my bed. I need to pace to dilute my adrenaline right now, or I'll explode.

"Nico, don't you think it's a little unfair to intrude in my life like that?" I say, going straight to the point. "First the scene with Martin and now your comments about my friends. You playing jealous boyfriend is getting on my nerves."

"Hush!" he hisses.

"Nico, what are you-" A female voice chuckles softly in the background and realization hits me like a bucket of iced water.

"Who is there with you?" I ask in a slow, menacing tone, just because I can't help it. An ancestral rage is mounting inside of me, heating my cheeks, knotting my stomach, and making my heart beat out of control.

"Lisa, listen, I-" I hear more female chuckling that Nico's lame excuse won't be able to cover, whatever it is. I don't even hear what he says. Jealousy is a bad, bad beast and it's roaring its ugly head in my chest right now.

"Nico, how dare you text me while you're sharing your bed with some brat!" I shout into the phone.

"No, it's not like you think, love. Kate and I were just-"

"*Kate and you*? Is there a 'Kate and you'?" I press my hand to my stomach. I think I'm going to throw up.

"Come back to bed, stallion," says the brat. I bet she's enjoying this.

"Sssh, go back to sleep!" orders Nico, but it's too late. I've heard enough. I'm probably on the verge of a nervous breakdown, and I'm wondering how I will be able to take my next breath. All I want to do is bury my face in my pillow and drown in my own bitter tears.

"Nicolas," I say breathlessly into the phone, "don't you

ever text or call me again! I don't want to hear your voice anymore, ever. Do you understand?" I cut him off and collapse on my bed. I muffle a desperate scream into my pillow, cursing my stupidity, wondering if I've finally hit rock bottom. *They say that's when you start to come up again*, the little voice in my head whispers between my sobs.

SEVEN

I've never been gladder for my run than this morning. I barely closed my eyes last night, drifting in and out of a restless sleep while thoughts of Nico with the busty groupie hunted me. I finally gave up and dragged myself out of bed as soon as dawn broke into my room. Hopefully a good, sweaty run will help me get rid of this overload of adrenaline.

I cross Hyde Park's deserted gates. The air is particularly cold this morning, heavy with humidity and with the smell of wet earth. It rained all night. My lungs burn as I quicken my pace and my warm breath, coming out of my lips in white, controlled puffs, blends with the fog.

There's no way I'm going to go to Nico's stupid birthday party, I decide as I set into my usual rhythm in the silent park. But then, if I don't go, Penny will be disappointed. I'm sure she is looking forward to hanging out with Lallo. If I suddenly refuse to go, she'll ask me why I changed my mind, and I will have to confess that I called Nico in the middle of the night and caused myself a jealousy attack…

I hear another pair of trainers thudding behind me. There are never many people running so early in the morning and the couple of regulars I usually cross paths with are nowhere to be seen. Maybe it's because I'm a good hour earlier than my usual time. Keeping my pace, I take a big breath in and glance over my shoulder but the fog is too thick in this part of the park to clearly make out the shape of whoever's running behind me. All I can see is that it must be a guy, and it's probably a tall, built one.

My self-preservation instinct kicks in and my trainers push harder against the black wet asphalt. I feel I need to put as much distance as possible between myself and this guy but he's too fast and despite my regular training, my heart is pumping spasmodically. I'm soon out of breath: ice-cold panic runs up my spine. I sense the big hand grabbing my arm before I feel it and a violent shiver freezes all the blood in my veins.

"Lisa, for God's sake, stop!" the man orders, jerking me

back. He's panting, holding me against his wide chest that is raising and falling erratically.

I push against it with all my strength and look up. "What the hell, Nico! Are you insane?" I yell, resting my shaking palms against my pulsing temples. "Do you want to give me a heart attack?"

Nico releases me and puts his hands on his knees, takes a few deep breaths then straightens to his full height and frowns at me. "*You* are going to give me a bloody heart attack! Didn't you hear me calling your name?"

I shake my head and push my hand against my racing heart: thank God for my ribcage or it would have leapt right out of my chest. A few breaths later, I finally feel my blood flowing again. My shock turns into rage. "What the hell are you doing here? Are you following me?"

"You hung up on me and won't take my calls. You always run in Hyde Park on Wednesdays and I needed to see you," Nico says, shrugging.

My conversation with Monique flashes back into my mind and I mentally curse my predictability. "What do you want?" I'm being rude and I mean to be. Nico is an idiot and deserves nothing less. He takes a tentative step towards me but I hold up my hand in warning. "I'll ask you again, Nico. What do you want?"

He smirks. "I like it when you are all angry and bothered, amore. You may not realize it but there's a powerful energy that radiates from you right now. It's sexy as hell."

"You're such a jerk!" I yell, stomping my foot on the wet ground.

A soft chuckle rumbles from Nico's chest and his smile cuts through the fog like a ray of warm light, melting the layer of ice around my heart. Oh God, I can't believe I've just stomped my foot like a child. Why, oh why do I still react so strongly to my ex? Why does he have to be so impossibly gorgeous? His navy tracksuit bottoms sit low on his waist and his grey thermic top hugs his muscular upper body like a second skin.

I shake my head. "Nico, this is not the time to talk. I want to finish my run and I can't be late at work."

Nico slips a half-empty water bottle out of the back pocket of his tracksuit bottoms and takes a long drag. He exhales in relief. I swallow hard in my dry mouth. I never bring water with me when I go running. I usually don't need to drink when I'm out in the park, but this morning is another story.

"Want some?" Nico asks, shaking the bottle in front of me. I want to say no but I'd kill for a sip right now. I extend my arm and he hands me the bottle, brushing my hand with his, on purpose, I'm sure. I glare at him while I take a big gulp. "Can I run with you?"

"No."

"I won't bother you, I promise."

I roll my eyes and push the empty bottle back into his hand. I won't be able to get rid of Nico this morning, I can see it in his eyes.

"Do as you please," I mumble, slowly resuming my jogging. My legs hurt; thank you very much, Nico.

He falls into step with me and we jog side by side, our silence broken only by the occasional bird that makes his presence known. Every few steps Nico's elbow brushes my upper arm and despite my anger, the contact sends a rush of electricity through my body. Damn him!

"You're special to me, love," Nico says, suddenly. "Whatever happens, never doubt that."

My head snaps to face him. "What the hell is that supposed to mean?" I ask, breaking my jog into a walk and stopping; so much so for maintaining a steady rhythm, as the trainer at my former gym recommended.

Nico puts his hands on his narrow hips. "It means that you'll always be above and beyond any other woman."

I stare up at him. "Why do you do this to me, Nico?" Why does he come and go in and out of my life as he pleases? Why do I let him? Despair builds at the bottom of my throat and my vision blurs.

"No, amore, please don't cry," Nico says, covering the distance between us. He wraps his arms around me and, after all, I still feel it, that sense of belonging I'm always craving for.

My arms lock around his neck on their own account; his scent invades my nostrils and his soothing words subdue my soundless sobs.

"You crazy, crazy girl," he says, tucking a strand of hair behind my ear. "You know, you shouldn't run on your own so early in the morning. This park is almost deserted."

"Yeah, you never know what sort of Italian jerks may cross your path."

"I guess I deserved that."

"Would you wake up at 6am three days a week and run with me?" I ask, looking up at his pout.

"Hell, no!" I push against his chest but his hold around me tightens. "But if we lived together, I'd make sure you got your morning exercise without leaving our bed," he says in a husky voice. My tired legs wobble at the intense sensation of his warm, soft lips on the sensitive skin of my neck. Does he mean that he wants to be back with me? *Don't ask him, Lisa: you know he doesn't.*

"Are you and this Kate together?" This shouldn't be any of my business, really, but I need to know what's going on between Nico and that girl.

"No. Let's go home now," Nico says, steering me towards the park gates and, once again, I go willingly, because I need him, dammit.

I'm teetering on the edge between pleasure, despair, and insanity: one more gust and I'll lose my balance, freefalling God knows where.

EIGHT

I need to find *that* present for Nico; the one he will adore and that will melt his pout into a grin.

This isn't going to be easy and I can't ask any of my girlfriends for help, especially Penny. It would be kind of embarrassing to give away how much I still care for my ex, the guy she's trying so hard to make me forget. The fact is that Nico is much more than my former boyfriend to me.

Nico and I grew up together, went to school together, and moved to London together; we were *together* for a long time. He was my first and only man. We're not in a relationship right now and maybe he's no longer in love with me, but in my heart of hearts, I know that our bond is still strong and it will never be completely cut. My girlfriends just wouldn't understand if I asked them to go shopping with me for Nico's birthday present.

I decide to ask Lallo for help instead. I'm meeting with him for lunch today. His day job is at a music store just two tube stops south from where my office is.

Lallo is a fantastic musician. Nico offered to refer him at the music school where he gives guitar classes, but Lallo declined, saying he wouldn't be a good teacher. I must agree that he kind of lacks a bit in the communication department; he's always been the quiet one among us three.

I step into the café and there he is, with his signature white trainers, blue jeans and black Korean-style jacket. "Lallo," I say, waving at him. "How are you doing?"

A hint of a smile touches Lallo's lips when his dark eyes zero on me. He stands up and gives me a quick side hug. For some reason, our hugs have been awkward since we were twelve. I blame puberty. "Hey," he says, "I'm good. You?"

"Great thanks! Never been better," I lie, just in case Lallo reports our conversation to his best friend. "Shall we have a look at the menu and order?"

Lallo nods.

"Ew, tuna!" I say, as soon as the waiter leaves us. "What is it with you and tuna? Do you really need to eat it every day?"

Lallo bites back a smile and takes a sip of his water. "You are not the only routine-bound person in London, you know," he says, and I roll my eyes at that truth. The waiter comes back with my Coke and disappears again.

"How are things at the store?"

"Good," he says, without elaborating. Words are not Lallo's preferred mean of communication but when he lets his drums speak for him, I swear that he can make you shiver.

"Is the tap working okay?"

"Yes, thanks again for fixing that. Penny sings your praises every time she washes the dishes!" I say, winking. Am I being too obvious? Lallo doesn't take my rudimental bait. He just sits quietly in front of me, his expression unchanged. That's too bad: I'm dying to know what he thinks of Penny. I think she might like him and it's so rare for my girlfriend to have an interest in anything besides her big thick books.

"So, Lallo," I start, clasping my hands in front of me on the little table: time is running short. "I need your help, please. I want to buy a special present for Nico for his birthday this year, something that he'll really like, but apart from a Jim Morrison-signed guitar that I wouldn't be able to afford even if it existed, I'm short of ideas here."

Lallo stares at me with his deep, dark eyes and I lose myself in their warmth. They remind me of the summer nights in Tuscany when we were children. On the night of August 10th, on Saint Lawrence's day or San Lorenzo, how we call it in Italy Lallo, Nico, my grandma, and I would climb up the hill behind my grandma's farm, with only the moonlight guiding our steps. Then we would sit quietly by the big oak tree, waiting impatiently to spot any falling stars. "Make a wish," my grandma would say softly, every time one of us would point excitedly at the pitch black sky. I drift back to the here and now and I find Lallo still staring at me in silence.

The waiter brings our food and I actually welcome the interruption. Lallo doesn't stare that long, I know him. He looks at you sideways for a while then loses interest. I wonder what's up with him today. Is he okay? The question is just about to leave my mouth when he finally speaks.

"Okay, I'll try to help you," he says, biting into his sandwich.

I sigh in relief, digging into my Caesar salad. "I was thinking, what about a new guitar, if not a Jim Morrison one? I could call into the store tonight and maybe you could give me a hand choosing one? You know I don't know much about music and-"

"No."

"Why not?"

Lallo ponders while munching on his tuna sandwich. "A music instrument is sacred for a musician. He needs to choose it himself, to feel comfortable with it."

"All right, that's not an option then," I say, rubbing my forehead. This is more difficult than I thought. "What about a jacket?"

"No clothing. You are nobody's mother."

"Well, okay… what about a city break?" I say excitedly, clapping my hands.

Lallo shakes his head slowly and drops his half-eaten sandwich into his plate as if it had suddenly turned into something disgusting. "I don't think this is a good idea," he says in a low voice. I actually wonder if he's talking to me or to himself right now. His eyes are cast down and he looks lost in his thoughts.

"But why not? This is a great idea! I could buy a low-cost flight to go somewhere nice, like Paris or Madrid! Nico and I could spend a romantic weekend together-"

"I said no!" Lallo says, startling me and the people sitting closest to our table.

"What's wrong with you today? You're not being yourself. Are you in trouble or something?"

"I'm sorry, Lisa. I just…I can't believe that he's still able to draw all your attention like this," Lallo growls. "He's a damn black hole. Can't you see he doesn't love you? What does he have to do for you to understand, do one of the groupies right in front of you?"

I gape at Lallo. His raw words shake me; they open a

scratch in my heart and I blink rapidly to keep my composure. I slowly push my salad away from me; I've suddenly lost my appetite.

"Lisa, look at me," he says, but I'm too busy keeping my tears at bay.

Lallo throws his napkin into his plate. "Elisabetta, I beg you, look at me. Can't you see?"

I look at the man in front of me I mean, I *really* look at him. His chest is rising and falling with every elaborate breath, his curly hair just touching his broad shoulders. His fists are clenched on the table between us and his eyes are searching my face, as if in a secret plea. Frustration and something I can't quite grasp ooze from him like a desperate mix, ready to explode. Oh my God, am I misunderstanding? No, it can't be…my heart starts to gallop in my chest.

I speak slowly I feel I'm treading on eggshells. "Lallo, I may be reading this completely wrong, and if I am, I apologize in advance for-"

"I think you're reading this completely right," he says, a sad smile curving his lips.

"But we…how… how long have you…"

Lallo leans forward and his voice drops down to a whisper. "Loved you more than anybody and anything else, even my damned music? Watched helplessly from the side how badly Nico treated you? Well, long enough to be fed up."

This is your childhood friend, Nico's best friend, I tell myself, but it's too late. He's now the man who confessed that he loves me, and after today I will never be able to look at him like before.

"Lisa, look, I'm sorry. Coming here today was a mistake. I just thought you wanted to spend some time with me, but of course this had to be about Nico," Lallo says and the sadness in his voice makes me want to run around the table and hug him tight. "Don't take me wrong, you know I love him. God, he's my best friend; he has always been and always will be. It's just that… Listen, I'm sorry, okay? Just forget what I told you. Jesus Christ, this is so messed up."

I take Lallo's hand in mine. Maybe it's a mistake but I can't help but making physical contact with him now. I can't stand seeing Lallo so uncomfortable and hurt, knowing that I'm the cause of his pain.

"Lallo, please, don't apologize. You have no reason to. I'm the one who's sorry for being so insensitive. I just didn't realize. I mean, with all the time we've spent together… I know you're right, I know Nico is not good for me, but-"

"You can't stay away from him," Lallo says, with such resignation in his voice that my eyes water. "Please, don't cry," he says, squeezing my hand. "I love you and I'll always be there for you. I just hope that you'll find somebody who truly loves you above all, as you deserve; somebody worth fighting for."

Lallo walks me back to my office. He talks about the shop, trying to make it less uncomfortable for me. He assures me that it's fine with him that we're only going to be friends, but I have a feeling that his words are just words of pride. Either way, I selfishly hope we'll stay as close friends as we've always been. What would I do without him in my life?

We say goodbye and he sprints down the tube stairs, disappearing in the crowd.

I turn on my heel and head upstairs to my office with a heavy heart. How ironic: Lallo wants me and I want Nico. What a trio. This is one situation I would never have thought to find myself in. The problem is that I don't see any solution to this. I obviously have no control over my feelings, how am I supposed to help Lallo handle his? He said he'll always be there for me, but who's going to be there for him? Who does one turn to when his best friend is his rival in love?

The elevator doors finally slide open. I walk briskly to my desk, immersed in my thoughts. In this big mess there's only one thing I'm one hundred per cent sure about there's no way I'm going to tell Penny about my lunch with Lallo. She doesn't need to know that she's the fourth ring in a chain of hopeless love.

NINE

It's Nico's birthday today; too bad that it was also an uneventful day at work, with plenty of time to fantasize about tonight.

I've been playing with it in my mind all day, what I'm going to say when I see Nico, the huge smile that is going to split his face in half when he unwraps his present, the warmth of his touch on my bare shoulders when he thanks me and the promise of a hot night together in his eyes. Tonight is going to be a memorable one.

I sigh, resuming threading my brush through my blond tresses. Penny's standing next to me, making faces at our big bathroom mirror, as she always does when she applies her lip gloss, and I bite back a chuckle. It feels good to not have to hide that I'm seeing Nico, for once. At the same time, I'm trying to not look too enthusiastic about the party, although inside I can't wait to see my ex.

Penny's phone rings: it's that ringtone again, the one she never answers. Who's calling her?

"Did you change your phone's ringtone?" I ask, tentatively. I know, I suck at prying.

She lets the call go onto voicemail, without sparing the screen a glance. "No, I didn't."

"It sounds different."

"It's a ringtone for somebody annoying, so that I know immediately that he's calling."

Ah-ha! "*He?*" I ask. "Who's *he?*" Penny gives me a look and walks past me. "All right, all right. Keep your dirty secrets for yourself, Penny Garcia," I say teasingly, and when that doesn't entice a reaction from my friend, I just shrug a shoulder. She'll tell me about this guy when she's ready.

I gather scissors, tape, and paper to wrap up Nico's present. I sit down at the kitchen table and unfold the baby-blue birthday paper, flattening it gently with my palms. I carefully position the wooden box in the center of the paper and set to work.

After my lunch with Lallo the other day, it felt wrong to buy any of the things that he dismissed so I racked my brains until I found something completely different: a bottle of vintage Port.

I don't particularly like alcohol but this is supposed to be a good, collectible piece. It cost me a fortune but it was bottled the year that Nico was born, a personal touch that I'm sure he'll like.

The outfit I'm wearing underneath my clothes, straight from Victoria Secret's store in Bond Street, is my other gift to Nico; that is, if things go as I plan. It's unwise, and I'll probably end up regretting it as I've regretted every single time with Nico over the last five months, but the truth is that I wouldn't mind spending the night with the birthday boy. My pulse accelerates instantly at that thought and I have to shake my hands before resuming cutting the paper. I'm hopeless, I know.

Penny walks into the kitchen, squeezing an old stress ball that she brought with her when she moved in with me. "Wow, you look stunning, Chica!"

"You think so?" Penny asks cautiously, skimming a hand over her black skirt. I can't help noticing that it's at least three inches shorter than the usual length she wears. "Look at those legs! Where were you hiding them? You'll have to beat guys away with a stick tonight!"

"Ah, shut up!" she says. She throws the stress ball at me and it hits me on the side of the head.

"Hey! Don't turn violent on me now. I just meant to give you a compliment."

"Do you really think I look okay? Isn't this too short?" she asks, tugging at the hem of her mini-skirt. I stare at my overconfident lawyer girlfriend. I can't believe she's uncomfortable in a mini-skirt. What's wrong with her tonight?

"Penny, your skirt is perfect. You've got a killer body walking under that big brain, girl. You should go out more and show it off."

"Ha! Speaks the one that would rather grow old on that sad green couch than leave the apartment," she says, pointing an accusing finger at my favorite piece of furniture.

I sigh. Penny's right, of course. "All right," I say, pushing myself up to stand, "point taken, but I've been trying to make an effort, you know."

"Whoa, I can see that!" my friend says, her eyes going wide; then her expression changes. She braces her hands on her hips and glares at me.

"What?" I ask, following her gaze down to my red strapless top, black leather leggings and sexy black boots. "You didn't expect me to dress like a nun, did you? We're going to a rocker's birthday's party, not to church!"

"Exacto, it's *Nico's* party we are going to."

"What do you mean?" I ask flatly, but my heart is racing from playing dumb. I hate getting busted.

Penny exhales heavily. "Whatever. Just remember that you have a date with Nancy's guy on Saturday."

"Well, I guess I do, if he doesn't chicken out again," I say dismissively, turning the wrapped box upside down to stick on another piece of tape.

Penny rolls her eyes. "Let's give the guy the benefit of the doubt, shall we?"

"Of course, Mrs. Lawyer," I say, sliding the now wrapped box to the edge of the table. "Can we go now?"

"We can. Nice present, by the way. Too bad that Nico doesn't deserve it."

I stare at the blue box and debate with my practical side one last time if I should bring it with me to the club or not. It's going to be crowded there, but I know Nico: he'll want to make a toast and sip the old Port with his closest friends. Yes, I decide, I'm going to give him the bottle tonight.

We arrive at the fancy club in Westminster that Nico has chosen as his party venue. There's a long queue of people waiting to get in and three huge bouncers in black, filtering them. I text Lallo that we're outside; a couple of minutes later, he slides out of the door and walks around the bouncers.

He takes me in, then Penny; then he glances at the door and then back at me. He looks nervous, as if he's hiding something. I know one thing or two about hiding how you feel.

"Let's go inside," Penny finally says. Her voice is unusually pitched: is it for Lallo that she's gone out of her comfort zone and worn her little black skirt? As on cue, she rests her hand in the crock of his arm and I smile to myself. She really likes him. They are two very special human beings; they'd make a fantastic couple. I just hope that Lallo will open up to Penny and come to appreciate her.

There's a human wall beyond the club door and the music is deafening. I set Nico's present on my hip, holding it in place firmly. Penny wraps both her arms around one of Lallo's while I instinctively reach out for his other hand. His fingers squeeze mine gently and he tugs us forward with him, shouldering his way inside the club.

We stop at the bar for drinks. Lallo doesn't even ask me what I want; he just hands me a glass of soda and puts a colorful cocktail in Penny's hand before we resume the almost impossible mission of reaching Nico's party though the crowd.

I spot Jude, another Lost Souls band mate; he's laughing a belly laugh with each of his arms draped around a girl's neck. Freddie, the band's agent and Charlie, his assistant, are also there, drinking and obviously having a good time. Bruce, the Lost Souls' bass player, is dancing slowly nearby, snogging with a blonde I've never seen before.

I abandon my glass on a table and manage to slide out of my jacket, balancing Nico's present in my arms. "Where's Nico?" I ask over the music.

Lallo stops abruptly and turns to us. "Why don't you girls hit the dance floor? One of the best DJs in town is playing tonight."

"Come with us!" Penny says, pulling Lallo's arm, but he doesn't move an inch.

"I want to give Nico his present first," I say, pointing to the box on my hip.

Lallo looks over his shoulder then back at me and shakes his head.

"Lallo, let Lisa get rid of the box already and then we can go dance!"

Lallo hesitates then he steps to the side and I see it, what he's been trying to hide. Nico is sprawled on the sofa with a girl on his lap. They're tongue-kissing and his hand is squeezing her backside. My breath catches in my lungs. It's the brunette I saw sitting at the front table the night we went out with Danny and David, and I bet my butt her name is Kate.

I almost drop the box, partly from the shock, part intentionally, to destroy any physical evidence of the fact that I care about Nico, but I guess I can't conceal the horror in my face.

"What an idiot!" Penny yells. "Lisa, are you all right? I knew we shouldn't have come, I knew it! Let's get out of here!"

"No," I say, my eyes glued to Nico and the girl. She's rubbing against him now and he definitely doesn't look upset about that. A fast sequence of camera flashes illuminates their faces but they're obviously too busy swallowing each other's tongue to notice. I'm disgusted, but at the same time, for some reason I'm not able to take my eyes off their lips joined together, as if I *needed* to imprint in my mind the shocking image of Nico making out with another woman right in front of me. I take a deep breath in and order myself not to gag.

That's it, Lisa: that's what you knew he was doing when you weren't looking, but you tried with all your strength to push to the back of your mind. And now it's here, in full display for you, for the local press and for anybody else who may swing by. I know, I respond in my head. I tighten my shaking arms around Nico's present. I've never felt so stupid in my entire life, but I will not run away like a hurt little girl. I will not give him, or the brat he's with, that satisfaction.

"No, Penny. I'm not going yet. I want to give Nico his present before we go."

My friend shakes her head but I ignore her. I've come this far and now I'm going to play this my way. I won't be making a scene, oh no. I may be still pathetically in need of Nico's attention, but I know that technically he's not mine anymore so I have no right to play the jealous girlfriend, at least not in public. This won't stop me from making him feel bad about the way he's behaving in front of me though. He knew I'd be here tonight; he knew but he obviously doesn't give a damn.

I take a steadying breath and walk up to the sofa, waiting to be acknowledged. Nico's half-closed eyes go wide when he finally registers me and he instinctively pushes the brunette off his lap. The girl glares at me, obviously not happy about the interruption.

"Happy birthday!" I yell over the music, but it comes out like an accusation. Nico tries to sit straighter but it's a huge effort for him. Now that I'm closer, I can see why: he's absolutely, completely wasted. I drop the box on his lap and he winces. I guess this is not as soft and warm as Kate's fat rear, is it, Nico? I hiss in my head. Nico fumbles to unwrap the box. He finally manages to tear the paper and takes the bottle of vintage Port out. He blinks, trying to read the label, but he couldn't put two and two together in his state. "Thanks, love," he slurs, holding the bottle up.

The brunette snatches the bottle from his hand and yells, "More boooooze!"

"Back off, Kate," Nico drawls, trying to get hold of the bottle, but Kate's standing up now, swinging the bottle in front of his unfocused eyes.

"Hey, that's not yours! Put it down!" Penny yells, taking a step forward.

"And what are you gonna do about that?" Kate asks, smirking.

"Cut it out, Kate," Lallo says, but it's too late: one by one, Kate's long, ring-filled fingers leave the bottle until the vintage Port slips from her hand and crashes to the floor.

"Oops," she says, covering her smirk with one manicured hand. Nico is taking a long gulp of his beer on the sofa a few feet away, completely oblivious that his birthday present has just turned into a puddle of dark liquid and smashed glass. Don't cry, I order myself. Don't. You. Cry.

Somebody calls the staff and two guys come over to mop the floor, taking away what's left of my present and of my dignity.

In this loud mess of people and alcohol and music, I hear

an alarm sound loud and clear in my head. There's something quite disturbing about this Kate. You will think that I'm biased in this situation, and I probably am, but for some reason, I feel that this girl is negative to the core. She's one hundred percent trouble of the worst kind.

Nico takes a break from his beer for air and I lean forward, close to his face. "Nico, this girl is bad news, stay away from her," I tell him in Italian.

His lips twist in a drunken smile. "Don't be jealous, love. At the end of the day, you're the only woman I care about and one day, when all this is over," he drawls, waving to the party around us, "I will marry you." He reaches out for me but Kate takes his hands and somehow pulls him to his feet. He swings before he finds his balance, steadying himself on Kate's shoulders, He's far gone, but Kate is well planted on her stupidly high heels, the idiot.

"Lisa, let's go," Penny says.

Kate starts to drag Nico towards the back of the club, towards the toilets and an emergency exit. I grab Nico's arm instinctively. "Nico, don't go, you've drunk too much and she hasn't," I say in Italian.

"Whatever you're saying, just shut up!" Kate barks and pushes Nico forward.

"Nicolas, don't go!" I say louder, right into his ear. He laughs, waving me away. He's a drunken puppet in Kate's hands, however badly-intentioned, and my protective side kicks into overdrive. Kate pushes him another foot forward and I lose it, right there in the middle of the club. "Lallo! Lallo, please, stop them! He's drunk and he doesn't know what he's doing!" I scream desperately, shaking Lallo's arm.

Lallo looks undecided. He shifts on his feet as if two equal forces were pulling him on each side then he finally steps forward and grabs Nico's shoulder. He says something in his best friend's ear but Nico waves his hand to dismiss him, and follows Kate to the back of the club. Just before they disappear into the toilet, I see it: Kate's smug, triumphant smirk. My stomach churns and I brace my shaking arms around my middle. "I'm sorry, Lisa. He didn't want to listen."

Tears wet my heated cheeks; I didn't even realize I was crying. My concern for Nico blends with pain and a sense of defeat as I turn on my heel and head for the door.

TEN

"As painful as it was, it probably was for the best."

I stare at my mug and nod.

Two weeks have passed since Nico's birthday party but it feels like yesterday. The pain is still pulsing deep in my heart but Penny is right: I guess that was the wake-up call I needed. Now I can no longer ignore what I saw with my own eyes that Nico is absolutely, one hundred percent over me, over *us*. Oh, believe me, I've definitely learned my lesson in the dim light of that club. It was a long time coming.

Sometimes I wish I would listen to other people's warnings, learn from their words. I would be wiser and that would save me from a lot of pain. Unfortunately, that's not who I am. I have to make my own mistakes and accept the consequences.

"She's not even pretty," Penny says to console me. She's been incredibly supportive over the last couple of weeks, trying to cheer me up and shoving pints of disgusting, supposedly witch-powered, infusions down my throat to soothe my sorrow. I'm grateful that my friend has been trying to help. I don't know what I'd do without Penny, or Lallo.

I smile, thinking back at how Lallo protected me in the club, physically shielding me from what was happening on that sofa behind his back. If only I could love my friend like a woman loves a man, I'm sure Lallo would make me very happy… I blink in disbelief. Oh God, did I really just consider that? What kind of person am I to think about Lallo as more than a dear friend, knowing that Penny has an interest in him? I close my eyes, disgusted at myself, at the path my thoughts have just taken. I sit straighter in my chair. Is pain making me a bad person? Damn Nico for bringing the worst out in me! The list of things I blame my ex for just got longer. My glance settles on Penny and guilt washes over me.

She's staring at me, biting on her lower lip. "Where have you gone, Chica?"

"Uh?"

She exhales heavily. "All right, because I'm feeling generous today, I'll give you another week. If, by next Saturday, you're still zoning out on me while I'm talking to you, I swear I'll call an emergency meeting with the girls."

"That won't be necessary," I say, more out of pride than conviction.

"Well, it would certainly help you move on if you could have some sort of closure with this whole situation with Nico," Penny says, stirring her steaming coffee.

"That's gonna take much longer than two weeks, I guess, but I'm making progress. I actually spoke with Nico last night."

Penny's eyes go wide. "You finally did? I thought you'd never speak to him again!"

"That's impossible, Penny, and you know it. Nico's part of my life whether I want it or not, and I couldn't avoid him forever, anyway."

"What did he say?"

"He apologized."

"Well, I would hope so!"

"He said he was sorry about my present and that he feels responsible because if he hadn't been so wasted, 'the accident' with the bottle wouldn't have happened," I say, air-quoting.

"That surely wasn't an accident!" Penny says, outraged. "Is he playing dumb or what?"

I shake my head. "I told him that it was no accident, and so did Lallo."

"And?"

"Nico thinks that I'm accusing Kate of something she hasn't done because I'm jealous," I say, grimly.

"What an idiot! Everybody saw Kate drop the bottle on purpose!"

"Apparently, Nico doesn't believe me, or Lallo, for the matter. Lallo says that Nico deserves to think whatever he thinks and that it makes no difference really, but it still upsets me that Nico would believe that brat over me and his best friend."

"Yeah, it sucks," Penny mutters behind the rim of her mug then she sets it down on our kitchen table. "Look, Lisa," she says tentatively, "I was talking with Nancy yesterday and…we don't want to pressure you, but don't you think it's time that you went back to meeting new people?"

I look out of the window; it's a bright morning outside. I rub my forehead. I know that my friends are right. I can't hide forever.

"Jackson has been asking about you," Penny says, at length.

"He has?" I ask, surprised. Last time I checked, I was just another slot in his diary. "Why would he? I don't even know the guy."

"Well, you texted him that you'd get in touch several days ago. When he didn't hear from you, he asked Nancy if you were all right."

"How sweet," I say, but there's no sarcasm in my voice. On the contrary, I'm impressed.

"That's what I thought too. I think you should text him back and go out with him."

I press my palms against my tired eyes. I don't feel like texting anybody right now but maybe I should. I don't want Nancy to think that I've been avoiding her guy on purpose. She wouldn't be pleased.

"All right, I'm gonna text him," I say, snatching up my phone and hitting the keyboard quickly before I change my mind.

"Good girl," Penny says. She takes our empty cups from the table and places them in the sink.

I indulge in a long, hot shower and when I go back to my room to get dressed, I'm surprised to find a text from Jackson.

Hi Lisa. Yes I'm in London and yes, I still want to go out. What about dinner tonight?

Tonight? Who drops an invite to a stranger on such short notice? I plop down on my bed and bury my still-wet head under my pillow. Damn, I had plans for tonight! Three episodes of Together Forever, a big bag of popcorn and two chocolate bars. I'm pathetic, I know. I need to get a good grip on myself: it's the weekend and I texted Jackson first… I really don't think I can say no. What would Nancy think?

Me: Sure, tonight would work

His answer comes in a few moments later.

Jackson: Do you like Japanese?

Me: I love it

Jackson: Great, I'll text you back

He won't find a table anywhere good, I mumble to myself as I slide into my faded tracksuit bottoms and old warm jumper: Saturday night is the busiest night in London. I just hope that food poisoning won't be on tonight's agenda.

My phone beeps.

Table booked at Origami at 8pm. I'll pick you up at 7.30pm

I read Jackson's text again, then once again. Holy cow! Origami in Chelsea is one of the highest-rated Japanese restaurants in London. I tried to go there with my mum for a treat when she visited me last summer but there was at least a six-week waiting list for dinner time. Apparently the place is not only excellent, it's also tiny. How on earth did this guy manage to book a table for the same day? I send Jackson my address and waltz into the kitchen in a definitely better mood.

"Guess where I'm going tonight," I say, smugly.

Penny looks up from her huge book and beams. "Wherever that is, I already like who you're going with."

I call Nancy and she's so happy to hear that I'm finally going out with her guy that she manages to squeeze me into her busy afternoon schedule with virtually zero notice.

I spend a hyperactive afternoon cleaning the apartment until it is spotless and ironing like a possessed woman; well, maybe I'm just a bit nervous about tonight. To her utter surprise, I even iron Penny's stuff, until it's time to head to Nancy's. She welcomes me with open arms and immediately sets to washing my hair. Any of the girls who work for her could do that but when I go to Nancy, she won't let anybody else touch me. The salon is in full swing around me and I inhale deeply, loving the fresh smell of professional hair products.

"Are you looking forward to tonight?" Nancy asks, grinning.

"Of course I am." I'm genuinely thrilled, but I won't tell my friend that it's because I've been dreaming of putting my feet under one of Origami's tables for months, which has nothing to do with her referral, actually. That wouldn't be very nice.

"I'm glad that you decided to finally go out with Jack. He's an amazing guy."

An amazing guy, I repeat in my head. I'm taken aback: this is a strong statement, even for life-enthusiast Nancy. Actually, I think I've only heard her compliment a man so zealously when she spoke about her husband, John, before I met him for the first time. I'm suddenly curious about Jackson.

"How do you know him?"

"He's my cousin."

I sit straighter in my chair. "Jackson is your cousin?"

"His mum and mine are sisters," Nancy says, nonchalantly.

I stare at my friend's reflection in the mirror in front of us, startled. "Why didn't you tell me until now?"

Nancy shrugs. "I didn't want to push you too hard but now that you've gotten there on your own, there's no reason to not tell you, is there?"

"I guess there isn't," I say, curving my lips in the best nervous smile I can manage. The gears in my head are spinning like crazy and my palms are sweating. This may not be a big deal for Nancy, but it damn is for me! It's my friend's family territory I'm about to trespass on with this date, and I didn't expect that. If possible, this puts even more pressure on this whole blind dating thing. Just what I needed, I think to myself in panic.

But I have to confess that there's a place in my mind where a lively, healthy curiosity is blossoming. I may not be good at first dates, or relaxed around strangers, but I'm intrigued by people I don't know. Despite the fundamental risk of mingling with my friend's family, the idea of getting to know Nancy's cousin is appealing. An image of a male version of Nancy – tall, blond, with blue eyes – pops up in my head, disrupting my trail of thoughts.

"What does he look like?"

Nancy laughs. "I'm not gonna tell you. You'll meet him pretty soon, won't you?"

"Yes, but how am I going to recognize him when we finally meet?" I ask, batting my eyelashes.

"No need to recognize him, sweetie. I'm sure he's gonna pick you up."

My cheeks turn a darker shade of pink. "How do you know that? Has he told you?"

"Of course not! I just know my cousin; he would never have you meet him at some restaurant on your first date. Jack knows how to treat a lady, sweetheart. His mom and daddy made sure of that. I just wish he would find someone special, who would treat him like he deserves," Nancy says then bites her lip. I open my mouth to fish for more information but she's quick to change the subject. "Anyway, have you decided what you're gonna wear tonight?" she asks brightly.

"I think I'm gonna go for a simple black dress."

"Lovely. Let's leave this gorgeous blond hair down then, shall we?" she says, gently threading her fingers through my locks, and I instantly relax under her touch.

"Whatever you think works, Nancy. I'm literally in your hands, and forever grateful for that."

My friend chuckles softly and my eyes drift closed. I don't need to watch while she works: I trust her completely.

***

"You look gorgeous. Hot. This Jack won't know what hit him!"

"Thanks, Penny," I say, slipping into my black little dress and fumbling with the zip. "I really hope this guy's worth all the effort. Where's my stupid mascara?"

"Hey," my friend says, touching my shoulder gently, "what's wrong?"

I let my hands fall to my sides. "I just don't know what to expect from tonight. What if it goes very wrong, like my night out with Paco? Oh, sorry," I say immediately, registering the expression on Penny's face.

"Don't apologize, Chica. Paco behaved like a pig and you did the right thing rejecting his 'offer.' Don't let that, or your story with Nico, ruin your night out. It's a new date with a new guy. Just try to have a good time, okay?"

I exhale heavily. "I know you're right. I'll do my best." It's only fair that I put some effort into this. At the end of the day, it's thanks to Jackson that I'm finally going to have dinner at Origami. And just like that, my smile is back in place. "And what are you doing tonight?" I ask, pointing to the living room where Lallo is reading a book and munching on a bag of chips.

"Lallo's gonna help me go through some notes tonight," she says. I'm surprised: the band usually plays on Saturdays, but I prefer not to ask anything that has to do with Nico. Teasing Penny is much more fun.

I look at my friend and raise a brow.

"It's for my exam next week, I need to study," my friend says, defensively.

"Oh, I see, Lallo's gonna help you study. Of course, he's an expert in… what's your next exam? International Law Applied to Hot Italians?"

Penny rolls her eyes. "International Law Applied to the Environment. Anyway, he offered and I couldn't deny him the immense pleasure of spending Saturday night studying with me, could I now?"

"That would have been cruel," I say, and we burst out laughing.

Just then the door buzz goes off.

"Oh, he's early!" I shriek.

"I'll get it, you go finish putting your makeup on," Penny says, pushing my mascara tube in my hand. She shoves me into the bathroom and closes the door behind me.

This is going to take me two minutes: I like my makeup light. I apply a touch of purple eye-shadow on each eyelid; it makes my amber eyes stand out. Then I work some mascara on each eye and blink, satisfied with the result. A touch of clear lip gloss and I'm ready to go.

I smile at my reflection in the big bathroom mirror. I must confess that by now I'm looking forward to my date with Jack; maybe it's because Nancy is one of my favorite people and although I've never met the guy, as he is my friend's cousin, it's not like he's a complete stranger, is it? Maybe going out on this date tonight is not such a bad idea, after all.

"You'd better go now," I hear Penny say as I open the bathroom door. Her tone is polite but assertive.

"What's going on?" I ask, walking into our small living room, and I freeze. Nico is standing at our door, his pout firmly in place. I can tell he's mad but he's trying to keep his temper in check. A muscle in his jaw jumps when he sees me and by the time he's finished taking me in from head to toe, he's glaring at me.

"Going out tonight, amore?" he asks, dryly.

I frown. Is he playing jealous again? What the hell? "What are you doing here, Nico?"

Nico takes two steps into our living room. "I came to give that back," he says, pointing to the black leather jacket in Penny's hands. It's my jacket, the one I was wearing the night of his birthday. How weird, I had completely forgotten about it. I was so out of it that night that I thought I'd left it in the taxi. A wave of unease washes over me, like every single time I think back to that terrible night, but I block that thought firmly. This is certainly not the time to dwell in negative thoughts: Jack will be here any moment now.

"Thanks," I say curtly, my heart beating fast. I really don't want Nico to meet Jack.

"You can go now," Penny says, but Nico doesn't move an inch. He just stands there, staring at me.

"Can we talk?" he asks.

"No."

"Please."

I hate it: I absolutely hate it when Nico pulls his puppy eyes trick. I know he only does it to get what he wants but it touches a cord deep inside me, like with a mother when her baby cries.

"She's ready to go out, man," Lallo says, standing up. "Why don't you come back another time?"

Oh, I'd forgotten that Lallo was here. There's kindness and understanding in his voice: I just don't know whether it's for me or for Nico.

"I only want to talk to you for a minute," Nico says, stubbornly. His fingers clench and he shoves his fists deep into his pockets.

When Jackson arrives, Penny can stay with him a few minutes while Nico and I speak in my room, I tell myself; yes, she can keep him company for a few minutes while I take care of Nico. My mouth is opening to suggest just that when a deep voice says in an American accent, "Am I interrupting?"

My eyes dart over Nico's shoulder. There's a man there, a fine-looking one, leaning against the door. He's looking me straight in the eye and I blink in surprise. I know those eyes: they are the same baby-blue as Nancy's. Oh, God, how long has he been there? I wonder, holding my breath.

"Let's go, man," Lallo says, taking his gaze off Jack and walking towards Nico. He whispers something in Penny's ear and she nods then he gently steers Nico towards the door. Jack steps to the side to allow just enough space for them to get out. Nico turns one last time towards me before disappearing behind the door with Lallo. I don't think I've ever seen such a deep scowl on his face since I've known him.

"You must be Jackson," Penny says, bless her, while I stand in the middle of our living room, staring at Nancy's cousin, my good manners completely forgotten.

"In blood and flesh," he says, an easy grin curving his lips then he sobers up. "That was pretty intense. Do you still want to have dinner together?" he asks, looking at me. I glance at the old green couch sideways: this is it, it's my way out.

"Of course she does!" Penny says in a pitched voice. "She's been impatient all afternoon to have dinner with you!"

Immediately my cheeks turn crimson. Thank you very much, Penny, I hiss mentally, glaring at her. But she has a point: I've spent a considerable amount of time getting ready for this date and there's a charming man standing at my door, waiting for me. "Of course, let's go," I say, shrugging one shoulder. I snatch my black leather jacket from Penny's hands: I kind of feel like wearing it, just to have some sort of closure, I guess, or just out of spite.

"See you later, Penny," I call over my shoulder.

"Have fuuun!" she chants.

Jack and I step out of my building and I automatically head towards the subway station.

"Do you really wanna walk in those?" he asks, pointing at my high heels.

Of course I don't. What woman would? I eye the taxi lane across the street longingly. Jack smiles and takes my hand. "Let's take a cab," he says, but I barely hear him; I am completely absorbed by the sensation of his hand around mine. Whoa. It's big and warm and soothing, and I squeeze it.

Jack opens the car door for me and I slip onto the dark leather seat, releasing his hand reluctantly. With a surprisingly fluid movement for his big frame, he sits next to me and gives the cabbie directions to Origami.

I glance at Jack sideways. Who is this handsome man sitting next to me? He oozes confidence but there isn't a trace of arrogance in him. On the contrary, he's making sure my feet don't hurt in my shoes. Jack seems to hear the rhetorical question in my head. "I'm Jack, by the way," he says, extending his open hand to me. I shake it without hesitation, glad to have an excuse to touch him again. There's something comforting and at the same time compelling in his touch.

"I'm Lisa."

"Is that short for Elizabeth?"

"For Elisabetta: it's Elizabeth in Italian."

"Is it? My mother's name's Elizabeth," he says casually, but I hear a touch of surprise and delight in his voice. Are Jack and his mother close?

"Was that an admirer of yours up there in your apartment?" Jack asks, cutting though my thoughts. Oh, no. Two minutes into this date and I'm already about to talk about my ex. I'm actually surprised by Jack's bluntness but I can't blame him. After the little show we've just pulled in the living room, if I were in Jack's shoes, I'd be curious about Nico too; or I'd have just run in the opposite direction.

"That was my ex."

"He didn't look too happy."

"He just came to give me back my jacket."

"I thought he'd punch me right in the face. He certainly wanted to."

"I'm sorry, that was really awkward."

"Don't worry, I can defend myself," Jack says, a slow smile curving his lips. "Besides, any man in his right mind would have a hard time letting a woman like you go."

"A woman like me?" I ask in surprise. "But you don't know me."

"I don't, but my sight is perfect. You are stunning."

Heat spreads in my chest and colors my cheeks. I sit back on the leather seat and smile, silently thanking the night for concealing my blush. We ride in comfortable silence for a few minutes until I can no longer wait to ask. "Jack, I was wondering... how did you manage to get a table at Origami at such short notice?"

"I know the owner," he says nonchalantly, as if it wasn't a big deal. I turn to him but I can barely make out his elegant profile in the dark cab. Now I wish I'd taken a better look at him earlier. Too bad I was too distracted by Nico.

An image of my ex's unhappy face materializes in my head but I immediately give it a mental kick. Go away! I'll have plenty of time to replay what happened in slow-mode one hundred times, but right now I don't want to think about Nico.

My gaze trails back to Jack's silhouette. I think I want to try to know this guy better and have a good time with him tonight. Maybe this is what a new date is really about: sane curiosity about another human being. Well, I certainly have bags of it right now.

"Hey, are you with me?" Jack asks, bemused.

"Oh, did you say something?" His megawatt smile breaks through the darkness. Wow. I clear my throat. "I'm sorry, I'm told I tend to zone out. I'm usually not like that, it has just been happening lately, you know. If you see me do that again, would you mind bringing me back to planet Earth?"

Oh God, did I really just blabber out that idiocy?

"It will be my pleasure," Jack says, grinning.

The cab pulls up in front of Origami. "Here we are," Jack

says, He pays the cabby and helps me out of the black car. I welcome his touch again and I don't mind at all when he doesn't release my hand immediately.

We step into a small atrium. The walls are covered in shiny, deep red silk that my fingers immediately crave to touch. I feel like we've just stepped into a padded jewelry box, leaving big, busy London outside.

As soon as she acknowledges us, the girl at the small reception desk tilts her head forward in what looks like a respectful bow and disappears behind a red velvet curtain.

"Wow, even the foyer in this place is fascinating," I whisper, casually leaning onto Jack to sniff him; sneaky, I know, but I suddenly need to know more about this man. He smells fantastic, like clean man and sandal, and for that, I add ten points to my mental assessment of this date right here on the spot.

"It's a remarkable place, isn't it?" he says, following my gaze over the walls. "The silk was imported directly from Japan, like almost everything else in here, people included."

I'm just about to ask Jack one trillion questions when a woman appears from behind the curtain. She's dressed in what looks like a traditional Japanese gown. I'd place her in her late fifties but Asian women age so gracefully that she may well be a decade older.

She looks up at Jack and smiles. "Mr. Kendall, how are you? Long time, no see," she says, bowing her head slightly.

Jack mirrors her polite gesture. "Konbanhua, Mrs. Kobayashi. Thank you for finding a table for us tonight. Lisa and I are very grateful."

Hearing Jack's baritone voice saying my name for the first time sends shivers of delight down my spine, and I shake a little. Wow. I instinctively bow my head too and when I look up into Mrs. Kobayashi's black almond eyes, they are smiling at me. "Please, follow me," she says, softly. She stops in front of the only free table in the small restaurant and invites us to make ourselves comfortable. Jack pulls my chair out and I sit on the plush velvet seat.

"How do you know Mrs. Kobayashi?" I ask, leaning

forward as soon as she leaves us.

"This restaurant is owned by a big Japanese holding that is a client of my company's. The president of the holding was Mrs. Kobayashi's late husband. My first assignment in my company years ago was to take care of Kobayashi's interests in Europe; that's how I met his wife."

"And you speak Japanese?"

"Nah, not really. I lived with a Japanese guy for some time when I was in college. He taught me a few words, but most of them wouldn't be appropriate for a night out with a lady," he says, grinning, and I decide right now and here that Jack wears the best grin I've ever seen on a man's face.

"Did you study in Asia?"

"No, in Boston."

That rings a bell.

"Where in Boston?"

"Harvard," he says, unfolding his candid white napkin on his lap.

I blink to prevent my eyes from bulging out of my sockets. Oh God, I'm having dinner with a Harvard graduate! This is amazing. Now, you may think that I'm exaggerating this but let me explain. I've grown up with the myth of Harvard. People like me have seen it in American movies over and over again: the good, smart guy in the movie always graduates from Harvard, and ends up saving the world.

Feeling suddenly self-conscious, I busy myself with my napkin, hoping that Jack won't ask me where I studied. There's no way Milan's State University could compare with Harvard. Well, I guess just few universities in the world could, right?

"What's your major?"

"Computer Science applied to Economics," he says, as if he was saying 'yeah, I'll have another beer, thanks.' And that completely undoes me. I openly, unashamedly, stare at Jack in awe. He's a geek. Well, it will surely take me some time to get around that idea because trust me, this guy most definitely doesn't look like the stereotype of the geek. He's devilishly handsome with his exotic complexion, mesmerizing baby-blue eyes and a smile that makes you melt into a puddle. As if that wasn't enough, his stance is relaxed in a confident, effortlessly sexy way that makes my heart beat faster. I must confess that I'm shocked by the effect this man has had on me in the twenty minutes I've known him.

Why didn't Nancy give me a heads-up about her cousin being a Harvard grad? I would have done something to feel less inadequate, like, I don't know, read some books, browse Wikipedia, or anything else to refresh my general culture. I'm so going to scold my friend tomorrow.

"You are staring," Jack says, his grin right in place, and my sweaty palm jerks up to my flushed cheek. *No chance of playing it cool tonight, Lisa, is there?* No, I don't think so.

"I heard you work at GBG Insurance."

"How do you know that?" I ask in surprise.

"Nancy told me, when she gave me your number. I hope you don't mind."

"How unfair," I mumble under my breath. I can't believe that Nancy told Jack about me but refused to give me any hint on him.

"Why would that be unfair?"

Oh, he heard that. "Because when I asked Nancy about you, she acted all mysterious and said she wouldn't tell me, because I would be meeting you soon."

Jack leans forward and looks me straight in the eye. "So you asked about me?"

"Yes-no- I- I was just curious, you know. I'm not used to… *this*," I say, waving my hand between us.

"I see. And what would 'this' be?" he asks, mimicking my nervous waving. Now that I see him doing it, I realize how silly it must have looked and I cringe on my side of the table.

"Blind dating," I whisper, casting my glance down.

Jack chuckles. "That's good   I mean, that you are not used to *that*. I'd rather not go out with a chain blind-dater," he says, filling my glass.

I smile shyly. I like Jack. He seems easy-going and down to earth and he's good-looking in an unconventional kind of way. I never thought that I could find a man that would arouse my curiosity like Jack is doing so effortlessly right now, and certainly not while I'm fighting so hard to get out of the hole I slipped in deeply with Nico. But hey, here I am, having dinner with a new guy and enjoying it. Maybe I'm not completely hopeless.

I look into Jack's blue eyes. He's not at all like I thought Nancy's cousin would look. Actually, I've never met anybody like him before. I didn't even think this color combination was possible, but what do I know? I'm just a small town Italian girl living in cosmopolitan London.

In my own time, I come back from my little mental stroll and realize that I'm staring, again. Jack is staring back at me and looks amused.

"All right," he says, "let's get it out of the way: ask me." I keep my face straight, but I know I'm blushing, and I'm sure I get a shade pinker when I see Jack biting back a smile. "Go on, Lisa. If you want to know something about me, just ask. You didn't seem shy about asking questions one minute ago."

"All right," I say, shifting in my chair. "I was just wondering... what your background is."

Jack throws his head back and laughs a rich, belly laugh. It vibrates through me, touching a cord deep inside me that I didn't know was there. "That must be the most diplomatic way I've ever been asked how come my skin is dark but my eyes are light blue."

I blush deeper at his rephrasing but his genuine laugh is infectious and I end up chuckling, too. "Yeah, I'm not very direct, I guess."

"No problem, I'm direct enough for both of us," he says, shrugging one broad shoulder. "Anyway, my mother, Nancy's aunt, is the typical English rose: fair skin, blond hair, blue eyes just like Nancy. On the other side of my family, my father is half African-American and half Puerto Rican. So there you go, I took the best from both of them," he says in mock presumption, pointing both thumbs at himself.

I'll have to agree with that. Jack is tall, lean but built and he has a perfect smile that matches his white shirt, and that contrast of his mocha skin with his blue eyes... well, it's fascinating. He is fascinating.

Jack grins. "Thanks."

"Oh God, I actually said that out loud, didn't I?" I moan, pressing my hand to my big mouth.

"That I'm fascinating? Yes, you just did."

I groan and get busy reading the menu. A lovely waitress, also dressed in what I guess is traditional Japanese attire, shows up and asks what we'll have tonight. I'm relieved that Jack doesn't criticize my order. Well, actually I've ordered less than I did when I went out with Paco, just in case Jack's also food-phobic.

I close the menu and catch Jack searching my face. There's a question in his expression. "You can ask too, you know," I say, knowingly.

"Ask what?"

"What you've been wondering about," I say, threading my fingers through my blond locks. Jack's eyes trail down the length of my tresses and linger on my bare shoulders.

"All right, then. Aren't Italians all short, with black hair and dark eyes?"

I giggle like a little girl. I just can't help it. I can't believe my luck: I'm having dinner with a smart, handsome guy who shares my sense of humor. Well, Nancy did say we'd be a good match but I never thought…

"Hey, you're doing it again! I'll have to find a way to keep you engaged here and now at all times when you're with me," Jack says, his gaze setting on my lips.

"I'm quite sure you'll manage, somehow," I say, a little breathlessly.

"I'll do my best," he says, and never has such a simple sentence held so much promise.

Our food arrives and I'm happy to say I'm not disappointed. Everything tastes delicious and the presentation is the best I've ever seen. Jack tells me about his job as Strategic Client Director at Remington, Gibson & Partners. I recall his company: it's well known in the City for its terrific reputation in the consultancy field. I'm actually quite impressed that, being only in his late twenties, he already has so much responsibility. Jack is exactly Nico's age. Then again, he's a

Harvard grad, with all that comes with it, at least in the movies.

Fantasy and reality blend smoothly in the unconventional package that Jackson Kendall is. He smiles at me from across the table and I sigh in contentment, swallowing the last spoonful of my rich chocolate dessert.

ELEVEN

I can't believe what a fun night I had yesterday: the food was fantastic and the company... Well, the company also went above and beyond my expectations.

Jack was funny, charming, and embodied the quintessential gentleman in every way: he opened and closed doors for me, he made sure my glass was always full of water, he insisted on paying for both dinner and the cabs from and to the restaurant and...and he didn't try to kiss me.

I don't know much about first dates but after all the flirting that went on at the table, I actually thought he would make a move on me; or maybe I hoped he would, just a little bit. In reality I don't know how I would've reacted but my pride would have loved it if he had tried.

"So he didn't try to kiss you?" Penny asks, shoving a huge spoon into a bucket of vanilla ice-cream.

"Nope."

"Really?"

"Yes, really, and I'm actually relieved that he didn't. I mean, I don't know him. He's nice and all, but that doesn't mean that I'm ready to be physically involved with somebody."

"You mean with somebody that isn't Nico?"

I glare at my friend. "Now what was that for?"

"That's just to remind you that there's a whole world out there and you should make the most of it."

"I will, in my own time," I say, pushing my chin up.

Penny rolls her eyes. "All right, all right. It's your life, after all. Anyway, when are you seeing him again?"

I glance at my watch. "In about forty minutes," I say, smugly.

"No way!"

"Mmm hmm."

"All right," Penny says, standing up, "I'm gonna go cook some food before I ask you any more questions. I don't want you to be late. By the way, do you want to invite Jack for lunch? I'm gonna make tortilla with potatoes and onion."

"Oh, I love your tortilla! But no, thanks. We're going out. Will you be all right here on your own?"

"Lallo's coming over."

"More hard studying to do?" I ask, biting back a smile.

"Shut up and get under that shower!" Penny says, brandishing her spoon at me.

I check my phone while going through my closet and, sure enough, I find a text from Nico.

Nico: Did you have a good time, amore?

My heart jumps in my chest. How weird: in some irrational, perverse way, I feel like I cheated on Nico last night, just because I had dinner with another guy and had fun. I know, right?! I chastise myself. He is the cheater, Lisa, certainly not you! But do you know what strikes me most? When I went out with Paco, or Martin, I didn't feel so guilty. Maybe it's because I really enjoyed myself last night with Jack. Our night out felt like a real date.

I debate with myself whether I should reply to Nico's text or not. If I don't, he will probably call and I don't want to have to worry about that later, when I'm out with Jack.

Me: I had a great time

Nico: Come over here this afternoon. I miss you

A rush of adrenaline pushes through my veins. I wish I could laugh about Nico's attempt to control my life and at my automatic reaction to him, but I feel I'm still far from being emotionally independent from my ex. My history with him is way too recent and intense and the constant sexual innuendo in Nico's words makes it impossible for me to have a relaxed relationship with him.

Me: I can't, I need to go shopping for my wedding dress

Nico: ???

I smirk at Nico's confusion. Of course he doesn't remember. He would deserve being left hanging for an hour or two, just to keep him on his toes, but I don't have time.

Me: At your party you said we'd get married. Don't you remember?

Hopefully that will shut him up, I mumble to myself while I put on my earrings, but I'm obviously too optimistic.

Nico: Come over and we can discuss that and other things

Are you for real, Nico? I say aloud and shake my head. Why on earth am I even mentioning marriage to Nico? That feels wrong, even as a joke. My entire relationship with Nico has been a bad joke. And the way he's been treating me… retrospectively, I'm not even sure he has ever truly loved me and that feels very, very rough.

I drop my phone into my bag, slide my feet into my shoes, and walk into the kitchen. Penny's cooking and Lallo's scribbling on his notepad. He looks up when he sees me. "Hey."

"Hey, thanks for defusing the drama last night, I really appreciate it."

He shrugs. "Anytime. Did you have a good night out?"

"Yes, I did."

"That's all that matters."

There's a knock at the door and I rush to open it.

"Hi," Jack says, leaning down to kiss my cheek. Oh, wow. His eyes look even more striking in the daylight. I lean onto his chest and get lost in his embrace for a moment, savoring the sensation of his muscular arms wrapped around me. I hadn't realized that I had missed him until now.

Penny clears her throat behind me and I reluctantly open my eyes. "Hi Jackson, I'm Penelope," she says, extending her hand. "We didn't have a chance to introduce ourselves properly last night."

"It's a pleasure to meet you," Jack says in Spanish, shaking Penny's hand.

"You speak my language? This is cool! But I can't place your accent…"

"My father is originally from Puerto Rico."

"Oooooh Lisa, you're a very lucky girl, Chica!" Penny says, winking at me. I'm just about to ask my friend why when Lallo stands up and introduces himself too. I snatch up my bag and my jacket and we say our goodbyes. We step out of the building and into the cool day.

"What would you like to do today?" Jack asks.

"I don't know, you're the Londoner, aren't you?"

Jack laughs. "I'm no Londoner, actually, although I've been

living in London for two years now."

"Isn't your mum from here?"

"She's actually from Oxford, north-west of London; that's where I spent many summers when I was a kid."

"And where does your American accent come from? Did you grow up in Boston with Nancy?" There are so many questions I want to ask him that I've made a plan to pace them out during the day, so that Jack won't think I'm a stalker or something. I think he'd never tell me to mind my own business, he's far too kind.

"I'm actually from New York City. That's where I lived all my life, apart from when I went to college in Massachusetts."

We walk down to the tube through the tide of people exiting the station. The subway in London is as busy on weekends as it is on working days, and that never ceases to surprise me.

"What about a stroll in the park on this fine spring morning?" Jack asks, studying the colorful underground map. "Have you ever been to St James's Park?"

"Where is it?"

I follow his finger on the map until it stops on a green dot. "Between Mayfair and Piccadilly."

"Isn't it too cold for a walk in the park?"

"Come on, Lisa. I promise I'll keep you warm and I'll treat you to a hot chocolate afterwards," he says, hugging me. I nod against his chest, a stupid smile plastered on my lips. I've known this American guy for less than twenty-four hours and I'm already having a hard time saying no to him.

Jack buys two tickets, takes my hand, and leads me down to the platform.

***

London is a green city, in its own way. Most of the green is concentrated in a myriad of parks, big and small, all incredibly well kept. Today I discovered that St James's Park is a jewel among them.

I had a wonderful time exploring the peaceful pathways

with Jack. Despite the unexpected gusts of wind that ruffled my hair, I didn't feel the cold: Jack kept his promise, keeping me close to his side, and it felt fantastic. He hugs me often and tight and both my body and my soul deeply enjoy it, although I'm not used to it. Nico's never been like that with me. I guess he's just not the warm, affectionate type, but I had never realized that before, because I didn't have anybody to compare my ex with, I guess.

I'm starting to think that spending time with Jack could really accelerate my healing process. When I'm with him, I almost forget to think about Nico. In Jack's arms I'm like an alcoholic who forgets to drink. "I feel you're good for me," I say, stirring my hot chocolate.

"You think so?"

"Mmm hmm."

"I think you're good for me too, sweetheart," he says, his lips curving in an enigmatic smile. *I very much hope so.*

"Tell me more about yourself."

"There's nothing interesting to say, really." I don't particularly enjoy talking about myself. I'd rather listen to somebody else's story just because I know mine just too well already.

"I'll have to disagree with that," Jack says, tilting his head to the side. "You're Italian: you are interesting by birth."

"Yeah, right," I say, chuckling.

"Are your parents Italian too?"

"Yes, and so were my grandparents, and their parents, for all I know. You see? Pretty boring."

"Don't say that about yourself."

"Wow, you sound a lot like Penny now," I say, rolling my eyes.

"Why?"

"She can be very inquisitive sometimes, and quite bossy."

"I'm not bossy. I just want to know where you grew up and if wanting to know you better is a crime, then I'm irreparably guilty."

Jack's smile is kind and he seems genuinely eager to hear about me. Well, I may give in, just this once. What do I have to lose, after all? Worst case scenario, I'll bore the man to death and he'll run from the café and from me. Okay, I admit that my self-esteem could be higher: I blame that on Nico. "All right then, I'll tell you a little bit about me. Just make yourself comfortable."

Jack makes a scene to pat the cushion sitting on his side. Then he arranges it between his broad shoulders and the seatback of his bench and looks back at me. "Ready, now."

I look out of the window and let the memories come to me. "I was born and raised in a little town in the north of Italy, but my mother's family is originally from Tuscany. So, while you spent your summers in elegant Oxford, I would spend mine running barefoot in the Tuscan countryside.

"My grandmother had a farm on the hills just outside of Florence; every year, as soon as school was over, my parents would pack me up and send me to my grandma. She was a strong, wonderful woman, my nana: she always had a kind word for everybody and would never punish us kids, even when we deserved it. Her farm was fairy-like. It was built on a hillside by a crystal clear creek. The landscape is gentle in countryside Tuscany, you know; the grass is thick and feels tickly under your toes.

"I was a real tomboy back then and my best friends were two boys, Nicolas and Raffaello. They were just a couple of years older than me and we were always together: we were neighbors and went to the same school. Their parents also worked full time so my grandma would take us all in to spend the summer with her. The farm was pretty big, there was plenty of space for the three of us to roam and get in trouble... I'm sorry, I'm talking too much. I got lost in the memories," I say, self-consciously.

Jack is staring at me, as if he's studying me. "Is one of the two boys the Lallo I met earlier?" he asks at length.

"Yes."

"Is your other childhood friend your ex?"

I nod.

"Is he the reason why you didn't contact me to reschedule when I was stuck in Vienna and missed my flight?"

Touché. I just sit there, frozen on my chair, unable to answer Jack's last, unexpected question. Did I mention that this guy can be quite direct?

He shakes his head. "No wonder your ex is still chasing you. You ruined him."

My eyes go wide. "What do you mean I ruined him?"

"You set his benchmark, Lisa. But my guess is that he also set yours, and that may actually make my life easier in the longer run."

In the longer run? Whoa. My heart beats fast and I'm afraid to believe what I've just heard. Does Jack mean that he's interested in more than casual dating with me? I don't want to set my expectations too high too early. This is not even a date; it's just two people spending a lazy Sunday afternoon together, although right now I wish this *was* a date. Let's be honest, I actually don't even know what I want right now. But Jack's unexpected words of endearment touch me deeply and my vision blurs. "I… thanks so much, that's very nice of you. Sorry," I say, blinking rapidly.

"You really are a sweet girl, you know that?" Jack whispers, covering my hand with his big warm one. "Don't ever apologize for expressing how you feel around me."

I look up into Jack's incredible eyes. They remind me of the blue anise popsicles the boys and I couldn't get enough of when we were kids. My grandma would make them for us to cool us down during the long, hot summer afternoons. 'Here, have a piece of sky,' she would say, smiling tenderly.

I feel an incredible urgency to share a special moment with this man sitting here next to me, to create new memories: memories that are only mine and his. I reach out from my chair to hug him and he welcomes me onto his lap without hesitation, as if he'd been waiting for me. I push my chin up and he kisses my cheek softly, then the other one, then the spot at the side of my neck that is pulsing wildly. A shiver runs down my spine and I hold him even tighter.

"We have plenty of time," he says, his sweet, warm breath teasing my lips and my senses. Maybe it's Jack's strong arms around me, or maybe it's this new concept that's slowly blossoming in my head, that there could actually be happiness for me after Nico, that makes me feel comfortable for the first time in what feels like months. This is easy, drama-free time that I'm spending in this man's arms, and it feels fantastic.

"Are you comfy?" Jack asks as I dare to snuggle closer. This feels so new and so familiar at the same time.

I sigh in contentment. "I'm in heaven," I answer, dreamingly. A soft chuckle rumbles deep in his chest and vibrates through me. It feels delicious and right.

That's it, I think to myself. This is going to be the memory of me relaxing in Jack's arms for the first time, in the café of St James's Park in London.

TWELVE

"How on earth can Jack be single?" I ask Penny and myself aloud. The question has been hanging in my head since Jack and I went out together for the first time two weeks ago. "I mean, come on! He's sweet, funny, smart, charming-"

"I can't say about the rest, but charming yes, he certainly is, and polite," Penny says. She's sitting on the couch, mixing unidentified ingredients into a small bowl, while I wash the dishes. I really don't want to know what trick she's going to use the mix for.

"He's as cuddly as a teddy bear. When I'm around him all I want to do is squeeze him!" I say, wriggling my soapy fingers.

"Aww! Is it bad that that's not exactly the first thought that comes to my mind when I see Jack, or his eyes, or his broad shoulders-"

"Hey!"

Penny looks up from her bowl and smiles. "I thought the day would never come."

"What day?" I ask, eying her suspiciously.

"The day that you'd find a man other than Nico interesting."

"Well, Jack would be really hard to ignore, wouldn't he?"

"I'll have to agree with that."

"So why do you think he's single and letting his cousin setting him up with a stranger? I mean, really, I can see how women look at him and believe me, when we're out together, I'm no deterrent at all. I can't leave him for five minutes to go to the restroom before some girl is chatting him up, like the other night at the movies."

"What the hell?"

"I know, right?" I say, dropping another dish in the dish rack unceremoniously. "Anyway, my point is that he surely would have his pick of women if he only wanted."

"And so would you of men, if you only wanted."

I press my lips together; I know that Penny's right.

"Anyway, why does that matter? It seems to me that since

he met you, he might want only one woman."

Excitement warms my cheeks at the thought that a guy like Jack may find me interesting. I know, I know, I should nurture my self-esteem more. I guess that after too many years of swimming within the reef of my comfort zone by Nico's side, embracing another man's interest for me still feels new. "I don't know, Pen… I feel like there may be something more there, something about Jack's way of relating to women that I haven't grasped yet, as if something has held him back. This has been bugging me for days now and I can't think of why."

"Is this about the fact that you haven't kissed yet?"

"Maybe," I admit, reluctantly.

"Why don't you just ask Nancy why Jack doesn't have a girlfriend?"

"I wish I could! But she's made it quite clear from day one that she won't feed me any information about Jack, and I can understand that. She doesn't want to be involved because he's her cousin." As my own words leave my mouth, it occurs to me that if things between Jack and I go wrong, my friend might not take my side by default, as she would normally do under other circumstances. A shiver runs down my spine at the thought that the outcome of a potential relationship with Jack may jeopardize my friendship with Nancy. How much is actually at stake here?

"Well, if asking Nancy's not an option, then there's only one way to know: you'll have to ask Jack."

I shake my head. "I don't think that's a good idea; and anyway, I wouldn't even know what to say to him. It's just a feeling that I have."

"You should always trust your guts, Chica. Maybe something happened with some ex-girlfriend and he doesn't feel comfortable sharing it with you yet."

"Yeah, maybe… but I'm still unsure about asking him anything so private."

"Well, you don't need to ask him directly, you know. Just use your skills, oh queen of diplomacy."

I make a face and busy myself with rinsing the last few dishes. Maybe if I ask, Jack will tell me how he feels about relationships. Not that we're together or anything, but who knows what could be…what if he has commitment issues? Could that also be the reason why he's been avoiding kissing me? What we have is definitely more than a superficial acquaintance: we haven't known each other for long, but I know we're already beyond that. I can see that he's attracted to me and the flirting is getting more and more intense, but every time I let myself be drawn to him, he hints at the fact that we should take it slow. I'm not ready to sleep with him either, but I wouldn't mind his lips touching mine. Am I asking for too much?

I dry my hands with a clean kitchen cloth and throw it on the counter. I'm giving up on racking my brains over the man for now. In fact, I'm planning a lazy, uncomplicated night in with a snack tonight.

I plop onto the couch next to Penny, sighing in relief. Just as I'm unwrapping my chocolate bar, my smartphone comes to life in my lap.

Jack: How was your day, babe?

Oh, I love it when Jack calls me those sweet little names… I busy myself with answering, all my concerns gone, just like that.

Me: Long but productive. And how are you?

Jack: I wish you were here with me right now

Me: Aww. Where are you?

Jack: I'm home, lying on my recliner, thinking

Oh…

Me: what's in your mind tonight?

Jack: You

Mmm… I love flirty Jack. The intimate tone of his messages and the sweet milk chocolate melting in my mouth are a delicious combination. I lick my lips.

"Is that Jack texting you?" Penny asks.

"Mmm hmm," I answer, tucking my legs under myself. Penny yawns and waves good night, disappearing down the corridor. I snug my shoulders in my fleece blanket and make myself comfortable on the couch. My quiet night in has just turned into a virtual rendezvous with Jack, and I'm determined to make the most of it. He's not the only one of us who's able to tease. I can be quite bold when we aren't face to face.

Me: and what am I doing in your mind?

Jack: do you really wanna know, babe?

Me: Yes, I do

I wait for his answer with trepidation. It scares the hell out of me but it also excites me how easily Jack can keep me on my toes.

Jack: I'm lying on my back and you're covering me in kisses. Every inch of me

Holy cow! I sit straighter on the couch, my tiredness suddenly gone. An image of Jack's superb, naked body   or at least a projection of how I think his body looks underneath his clothes   forms in my head. My cheeks are on fire: thank God Penny's just gone to bed. She would have caught me in no time.

Should I play it safe or follow my instinct? I feel quite daring away from Jack's intense gaze. He makes me feel shy when he looks me straight in the eye but here, alone in the dim light of my living room, I feel daring and free.

Me: I wish I were there to make you feel good

I hit send and wait for Jack's answer. Three, five, ten excruciating minutes pass. When my chocolate bar is gone, I start biting on my lower lip. Have I gone a step too far? Stupid, stupid, stupid…Well, he started it after all, didn't he? Doubts assault me and my blood pumps faster in my veins with every further minute that passes, until my screen finally flashes again.

Jack: Oh, baby, you'd send me right to heaven. Sleep well, sweetheart x

Phew! Why do I always have to doubt myself?

It's two hours later when I finally manage to drift to sleep with a silly smile on my face.

THIRTEEN

"Hey man, pass me that screwdriver, will you? Yeah, that one, thanks. For Christ's sake, who knew that assembling a cot would be so bloody difficult?"

Nancy, Penny, Lallo, Jack, and I are all at Andy and Monique's place, helping Andy put together the nursery and preparing a surprise baby shower for Monique. She's out shopping with Denise this afternoon, completely unaware of what's going on in her apartment. I'm so glad Nancy invited Jack's 'extra pair of hands.' I love how the defined muscles in his arms ripple when he lifts a shutter or hammers shelves into the wall. I must confess that with all our recent hot texting, I can't take my eyes off him: he is slowly driving me crazy.

"Andy! No swearing in your baby's nursery!" Nancy says, sternly.

"I wasn't swearing!"

"All the same!"

"But he's not born yet!"

"Or *she* isn't," Penny says, throwing at Andy the pink balloon she's just tied. It bounces against Andy's wide chest with a dull thud and he groans, swearing again but under his breath this time to avoid Nancy's wrath.

"I heard you, Andrew O'Brien!"

"So did I," Penny says sweetly, earning a glare from Andy.

"Ladies, please. Just let the poor man be. He's just a little nervous, aren't you, Andy? I mean, who wouldn't be? He'll soon be a daddy," I say.

"But that's exactly what I mean! When he's a father, he'll have to lead by example. It's never too soon to start practicing."

"Oh, I'll lead by example all right! I'm already planning to take him to Croke Park to watch Dublin beat whatever other county will be in the final when we visit on St. Patrick's Day next year."

I throw my head back and laugh. The blue balloon I just inflated but not tied slips out of my fingers and lands flat on

Andy's face and I laugh so hard that my eyes moisten. "But Andy, the baby won't even be six months old then!"

"Didn't you hear what Nancy said? It's never too early!" he retorts.

We all laugh together and then go back to our tasks. What a fun afternoon this is turning out to be. The nursery's coming out really nicely: it's all white and delicate shades of yellow and green, a consequence of Monique and Andy's decision not to know the sex of their baby beforehand. But if it was up to Andy, he'd paint all the walls and the furniture in a bright, solid blue.

"Would you really prefer to have a boy, Andy?" I ask, tearing open another pack of balloons.

Andy holds the screwdriver mid-air and stares out of the window for a long moment. "I don't know. I mean, I think it'd be simpler for me to interact with a boy. I'd know how he thinks, you know. I'd be more able to help him grow up, I guess. Men are simpler than women."

"Amen." We all turn to Lallo. He'd been working in silence until now.

"What do you mean by that?" Penny asks.

"Just what Andy said; that we men are way simpler than women think we are. If you only knew how simply we really think beyond that curtain of complexity that is your interpretation of what you think we think, you wouldn't waste your time with the half of us who are just plain idiots," Lallo says, looking me straight in the eye.

"Damn right," Andy says, and just like that, the guys resume hammering, as if they hadn't just touched on one of the most controversial aspects of human coexistence: the difference between men and women. Ah, men!

I suddenly need to be anywhere else other than here, under Lallo's intense gaze. I know he means well but I don't need him reminding me at every occasion that Nico is a jerk. I shift on my knees and stand up. "I'd better go start the finger food in the kitchen. According to Denise's plan, they'll be back in less than one hour," I say, glancing at my watch.

"Go ahead, I'll take care of these," Penny says, taking the

bag of balloons from my hands.

"Do you need help, sweetie?" Nancy asks.

"I'll help. I'm finished with those shelves, anyway," Jack says, and my heart misses a beat.

"Thanks man, they look great," I hear Andy say as I leave the room with Jack trailing behind me. I head down the corridor for the kitchen, very aware of Jack's eyes on me. My pulse accelerates only at the thought that he left what he was doing to be in another room with me. That's crazy, right? What is he doing to me?

I wash and dry my hands and when I turn, Jack is closing the kitchen door behind him. He walks up to me and wraps his arms around me. "I couldn't wait to get you alone," he whispers.

Memories of our hot phone exchanges come back full force and I thrive in expectation, my friends in the other room completely forgotten. I lock my arms around Jack's neck and melt against his chest. He feels fantastic against me, so masculine and warm. He smells of his cologne and man, and I fight the urge to push myself up on tiptoe and crush my lips on his.

"Mmmh, baby, you feel amazing," Jack says in my hair, drawing slow circles on my back. "So sweet and sexy." He inhales deeply, slowly, then takes a step back and looks down at me with hooded eyes. And there it is again: whatever it is that holds Jack back when we are getting too close is straining to take control over his emotions right now: I sense it in Jack's stance. I just wish I knew what it was; maybe I could make it go away.

Jack unlocks my hands from behind his neck and holds them in his, against his chest. Enticed by the warmth of his body, my palms open like flowers in the sun, sliding of their own accord over the thin fabric of his fitted t-shirt. His breath catches and when I feel the erratic beat of his heart under my hand, his baby-blue eyes turn dark with need. "Lisa."

Jack slides his hands down my sides, sending a delicious shiver up my spine and right to the back of my neck that makes my eyes flutter closed. "Yes, Jack," I hear myself say in a voice so husky that I don't recognize it.

"Just this once." He leans down, eyes locked to my parted lips.

"Hey, Jack! Do you have the Philips screwdriver?" I jump out of Jack's arms just before the kitchen door bursts open. "Ha! There it is," Andy says, pointing at Jack's back pocket. I open the fridge and all but throw my head into it. The fresh air does little to cool my burning cheeks. I close the fridge and busy myself with putting together bread and cheese. I hear the guys talking behind me, but I can't make out what they're saying. I'm too flustered and a little shocked by my reaction to Jack. It's always so strong and physical; there's something about this American guy that makes my heart race. I usually don't feel like this... A moment later, I hear the door close and my breath catches in anticipation. I turn, but I'm all alone in the kitchen with my thoughts.

***

"Surpriiiise!" we all shout as Monique walks through her apartment door.

"Welcome back, my love," Andy says and hugs his emotional girlfriend tight. He leads Monique to the nursery and when her eyes set on the adorable white cot in the corner, she actually breaks into tears.

"Thanks so much, guys, this means the world to me. Thanks, honey," she says, smacking a loud kiss on her boyfriend's lips.

We eat and drink and chat and laugh, and all the time, I'm very aware of Jack's presence. Every time our eyes lock across the room, my heartbeat speeds up and I have to resist the urge to fill the distance between us, sit on his lap, and finish what we started earlier.

Monique is over the moon: her oohs and aahs fill the room with every new present she unwraps. She's looking in amazement at the cute hand-knitted all-in-one that Penny got for the baby when Andy clears his throat. "There's one last thing that I want you to have today."

"Honey, one more thing to fit into our little apartment and you and I will need to move out!"

Andy stares down at Monique, his lips set in a thin line. He's so pale that I'm concerned he's going to pass out. He takes a little velvet box out of his pocket and drops down on his knee.

"Oh my God!" Nancy, Denise, and I shriek in unison. Monique just stares at her boyfriend in shock.

"Monique Abigail Smyth," Andy says, opening the little box with big, trembling fingers, "no morning goes by without me looking in the mirror and wondering what I did to deserve your attention in the first place, when you could have anybody you want. You're so beautiful, and smart. I love you. I want to spend the rest of my life with you and with our baby. Will you make me the luckiest bastard on Earth and marry me?"

Through my blurred vision, I see a crying Monique bob her head and throw herself in Andy's arms. "She said yes!" he screams in surprise and we all applaud and cheer and hug Monique and Andy.

I wipe my eyes with the back of my hand. Jack is staring at me, his face closed in an unreadable expression that makes me blink. "Congratulations, man," he finally says, patting Andy's shoulder.

"Thanks, my friend. It's the luck of the Irish!"

"Nah, it's just love, I guess."

"It surely is. Now you're next!"

Jack stiffens and answers politely, but I can see that he's suddenly uncomfortable. Maybe he does have commitment issues after all, or he just doesn't believe in marriage.

One hour later we've cleaned up and we're ready to call it a day, so that poor Monique can rest.

"Ah, these bloody swollen feet!" she says as she hugs us all, one by one, at her apartment door. "Thank you so much again for everything, guys, you're the best!"

"Take care, darling," I tell her as I step out.

"We're gonna take the stairs," Nancy says, pushing Denise and Penny towards the staircase door. Lallo follows them. "We're gonna stop at the shop to buy drinks. John has ordered takeaway pizza. See you at my place in one hour."

My friends' voices fade down the staircase and silence falls in the dim landing. I look up at Jack. He's looking at me, his lips curved in an enigmatic smile. He pushes the elevator button but instead of shoving his hand back into his pocket, he tugs a lock of my unruly hair behind my ear.

"So soft," he whispers.

I close my hand over his and hold it tight at the side of my neck, where my pulse is beating fast. I hope he can feel how much he can move me, just with the simplest touch. His palm cups my nape, and my eyes flutter closed. I feel Jack stepping closer, his breath teasing my lips. My heart is racing out of control in expectation. That's what Jacks does to me: I'd better get used to it.

The elevator doors slide open and Jack suddenly retreats. I stifle a moan and when I open my eyes, they land on two elderly women. They shift to make space for Jack and me in the elevator and I sigh, savoring the soothing sensation of Jack's big hand on the small of my back.

We step out of the building and into the crowded street. Jack's hands are shoved deep in his pockets now: our little moment is gone. "Nice party up there," he says, smiling.

"Indeed. But poor Monique, she was exhausted!"

"Can't be easy to carry an extra person inside of you for nine months," Jack says. He's always so thoughtful.

"Yeah, but it's worth it. And she has Andy to share all the ups and downs of this special time."

"Yes she does, more than ever since this afternoon."

I want to ask Jack about himself, if he wants a family one day, but I don't dare. I wish I could be as open as he encouraged me to be with him from the very beginning.

He tilts his head back and stares into the dark sky. "It looks like it's gonna rain again soon."

"You never know in London."

He takes my hand and laces his fingers with mine. He's smiling down at me and I wonder what he's thinking. "My car is parked over there," he says, pointing to an alley off the big road we are walking down. We cross the street and Jack opens the door of a silver sports car for me. I slide into the car. It smells like leather and Jack, so delicious and sexy, just like him. He starts the car and a few moments later, we're heading north, towards Nancy's apartment.

"So, what do you think about what Lallo said? Do you agree?" I ask.

"That half of all men are plain idiots? Yeah, I'd have to agree with that."

"No," I say, laughing. "That men are simple creatures, after all."

"I agree that most men's way of thinking is pretty straight forward, but that doesn't mean that women can read them."

"If you mean that we can't read your thoughts, yeah, that's true, although I just wish we could."

"No, I mean that sometimes, when she looks at a man, a woman can't see what's staring right back at her. And that's not because she's not able to see, but simply because she just doesn't want to see."

Oh, Jack, if you only knew how very right you are, I think to myself while I tamper with the stereo system of his fancy car.

"Take your ex, for example." That stops my hand mid-air. I look up at Jack. He's staring at the road ahead, one hand on the steering wheel and the other one on the gearshift.

"What about him?"

"He's obviously not ready to let you go, but you just can't see that."

I roll my eyes. "Jack, how can you say that? You've met Nico only once, and for a few minutes. How do you know what he does or doesn't want?"

"Body language speaks volumes. And don't forget that I'm a man."

As if I could forget how very male you are, Jack… That's not the point, Lisa! Focus! "Well, even if you were right, Nico and I are done - finito."

Jack pulls over in front of a little grocery shop and shifts his intense gaze to me. His blue eyes look silver in the darkness of the car. "Are you, Lisa? Are you really done with your ex?"

I rub my forehead. Why is Jack asking me about Nico? My heart is pulsing in my throat right now and it's suddenly too warm in this small car. I cross my arms over my chest and look past Jack's shoulder. "Of course I am."

Jack stares at me for a long moment. "As I said, body language speaks volumes."

I let my arms fall onto my lap self-consciously. "Jack, I like you very much. You make me feel... I want you to know that you're special to me. I'm just not very good at dating and stuff. I- I haven't had much experience."

Jack takes a deep breath then his hand finds mine in my lap. "You're special to me too, baby; very. God, I want to bring this thing we have to the next level so bad but we need to take it slow until you figure out what you really want. I just don't wanna find myself playing gooseberry: been there, done that, and I didn't like it one bit. Do you see where I'm coming from?"

I want to tell Jack that I don't need time, that I've actually figured out what I want already, and it's him, all of him, but I just sit there, searching his beckoning face, itching to make his frown disappear. He leans closer and stamps the sweetest kiss on my forehead, and I just fall a little bit more for him.

"One step at a time," he whispers and gives me an open, reassuring smile that makes me melt right there in his car's passenger seat.

"One step at a time," I repeat, wrapping my arms tight around his waist.

"Now let's buy some Puerto Rican chorizo to put on top of our pizza. John loves it. I always bring him some when he's back after a long trip. This little shop has the best in London."

I unbuckle my seat belt and open the car door. Jack is right there to help me out of the car. "He's been away three weeks this time, right? I don't know how Nancy does it."

"She just loves her husband," he says, shrugging one shoulder, "but I can tell you, John has been growing weary of all this travelling, lately. He hates to be away from Nancy. I think that soon he'll just hire somebody to send around the country while he supervises operations in London. After you," he says, ever the gentlemen, opening the shop door for me.

We do our shopping in the lovely ethnic store and drive the short distance to Nancy and John's place. John answers the door. "'Bout time!" he booms, hands on his hips. "I thought you two had eloped to Vegas or something."

"John! Leave them alone!" Nancy says from down the hall. She strides up to us and wraps her arms around her husband's chest. "He's just grumpy because he's hungry."

"Of course I am! I haven't eaten for eight hours straight!"

"Aww, poor Johnny!"

"This is for you, man," Jack says, holding up our shopping bag.

John's pout opens in a knowing smile. "Thanks, cousin. God, I love this Puerto Rican stuff."

So do I, I think to myself, so do I.

FOURTEEN

Jack is not picking me up tonight: we are meeting at a gym close to his apartment for a salsa class. I can't wait for my dancing class tonight. I love salsa; I took lessons when I was younger although I haven't practiced in a long time. I'm looking forward to shaking my rusty legs after a long day of sitting at my desk.

I've been playing again and again in my head the conversation that Jack and I had in his car the other night. It made me realize even more how truly an amazing and insightful guy he is. I love how careful and considerate he is about our relationship, how he respects me, and wants to do the right thing.

Jack is holding back to give me time to finally come to terms with my past with Nico: I mean, how many men in his shoes would do that? He told me that I'm worth the wait and that makes me feel cherished. And the attraction between us… it's a burning fire that keeps me warm and feels natural and right.

Jack wants me as much as I want him and I'm secretly thrilled at the idea of driving him crazy. The thought that his passion for me may be so intense that it could push him to pull free from the chains of his self-imposed restraint really turns me on. I must confess that I itch to see his raw, primal self. That's rather insensible of me, I guess, but it's just one of those selfish, self-comforting thoughts that a girl nurtures from time to time: like the thought that one day Nico will regret dumping me and will crawl to me and apologize profusely, only for me to say that it's too little, too late.

I decide to send a quick text to Jack. I'm counting the minutes until I see him again.

Hi handsome, looking forward to seeing your moves tonight

I tap my foot nervously. I'm always afraid I may come through too strong but then again, it was Jack who encouraged me to open up to him so I push my hesitation aside and hit send.

My phone's screen flashes almost immediately.

Jackson: I can't wait to see you and feel your body against mine

Whoa! I do a little victory dance and press my palm to my burning cheek.

Jackson: Everybody's heading to a club after class. Are you up for it?

Me: Of course

Jackson: Cool, see you later, gorgeous. Save a dance for me ;)

You can count on it, Jack! I jump on my bed, throwing my arms in the air; yes, like a child, and I don't care. I haven't been in a salsa club since I was eighteen or nineteen. A night out dancing to my favorite music with sexy-as-sin Jack? Yes, thank you!

I pack my gym bag with a pair of skinny jeans, a cute top, and high heels for the club later tonight then I rush into the kitchen. "Penny, do you wanna go salsa dancing tonight?"

"Going with Jack?"

"Yep."

"You see? I told you that you were lucky! Isn't that a nice perk of dating a Puerto Rican? Ninety-nine percent of them can dance."

I grin. A guy who can dance? Very nice perk indeed. "Does that mean that you're coming with us?"

"Nah, thanks, I'm going out."

"Where are you going?" Penny rarely goes out and I will not miss this opportunity to be nosy with her. Her lips curve in a small, apologetic smile.

"The band is playing at the Black Eagle in Soho."

The Black Eagle? Oh, that's the pub of 'the Martin incident': I guess this explains why, that disgraceful night, Nico and Lallo were there in the first place. To my own surprise, I register the information without blinking or feeling sad. I quickly check on my heart: it's doing fine, beating steadily in my chest. I smile, happy with myself.

Only a few months ago, I would have never missed a concert of The Lost Souls. Back then nothing was more important than spending the night watching Nico perform for his fans. But tonight it just feels natural that I'm not going to be there, that I'm going to be somewhere else with somebody else. Maybe I'm finally getting used to the idea that Nico and I have parted ways. My ex is too, after all. He's calling and texting me less, although things between us are still kind of overcharged.

All in all, I'm more optimistic about my future than I've been in a long time, and I know I should thank Jack for that. I just wish things with Nico could be more relaxed, evolving towards a true friendship. Maybe one day Nico and I will be just good, old friends who grew up together.

One step at a time, Lisa.

***

I arrive at the gym and ask for the salsa class. The receptionist points me to a big room at the back of the gym, where 'the popular classes are held,' she says, winking. As I cross the open space, walking around modern machines and sweaty people, I remind myself that I have a secret mission tonight. I want to know more about Jack and his history with women.

I reach the salsa room and swing the door open.

The room is crowded: there are at least twenty women and only around ten guys, and I'm not surprised at all. What is it with women and dancing? I remember when I took my first class years ago: the only guy in the group would be passed from one girl to another like a baton. It's not like he minded, though. I suspect that being the only guy in a bunch of excited girls was actually the real reason why he joined the class in the first place. In fact, he didn't miss one class, even the night that it snowed heavily.

I smile at that memory as I search the room for Jack, but he's nowhere to be seen. Uh, it's very warm in here and I slide out of my hoodie straightaway; half of the men are bare-chested anyway.

Two girls are trying the basic salsa steps in a corner. I walk up to them and observe their feet move, trying to remember how it's done. "Hi, do you mind if I watch?" I ask.

"Hi! Not at all," says the taller girl, smiling back at me.

"Hey, no problem," says the other one, giggling. "Just don't expect to learn anything good from us." Their moves do look uncertain, as if they were walking on burning coal, and I bite back a smile. I think I'll do better than that even after many years without dancing.

"We are terrible!" says the taller girl and bursts out laughing.

"Ah, you'll see, you'll get better with time," I offer, smiling.

"Thank you, but I don't particularly care," she says, shrugging one shoulder.

The other girl leans closer to me and says, "We only attend this class because the teachers are sexy to die for, and I bet most of the women and half of the men are here just for that too."

The other girl nods knowingly just as I hear clapping hands and cheering.

"Good evening, ladies and gentlemen. How are you doing tonight?" Jack says, causing more cheering and whistling. Oh, my God. My mouth waters: he's wearing a pair of faded jeans that sit low on his narrow hips, a white, fitted polo shirt with the name of the gym embroidered on the chest, and a big smile that turns into a grin when he finds my eyes across the room. I smile back at him, my heart beating faster in my chest.

"All right, everybody, who was here last week, please raise your hands."

Everybody does, except me and another guy. Yes, this class is quite popular indeed.

"Thanks, folks. For those who don't know me, my name is Jack and this is Julio," he says, patting the guy standing next to him on the shoulder. He's shorter that Jack, with a more definite Latino look, and he's also sporting the gym's white polo shirt.

"Now, as you can see, my feet are bare tonight," Jack says, pointing to his bare toes at the other end of his faded jeans. God, his feet! Is there a part of him that isn't sexy? "That's for you to be careful not to step on my feet and to remember which one of your feet goes where with every step. Well, Julio isn't such a committed teacher, obviously," Jack says, looking pointedly at Julio's flashy yellow trainers. The room laughs and the class begins.

The atmosphere in the room is positive and relaxed, so much like Jack is. Everybody is learning and having a good time, moving as well as they can to the rhythm of the salsa music playing in the background. Some of the girls have a particularly good time when Jack and Julio ditch their polo shirts and give them an individual demonstration of the steps. I ogle at Jack sideways: with his impressive pecks and six-pack in full display, he looks good enough to eat. One of the girls sets her hand just where Jack's lower back curves into his gravity-defying butt and I miss a step. I'm pretty sure that hand should go on Jack's shoulder, instead. I'm also pretty sure that I'm jealous, and the intensity of my feeling catches me by surprise.

"Sorry," I say, absently. I'm paired with an English guy, who's having a hard time reproducing the very basic salsa step that Jack has just demonstrated, and I've just stepped on his foot.

"No problem."

Jack moves the girl's offending hand back to his shoulder and I sigh in relief, finally focusing my attention on avoiding injuring my dancing partner. God, this guy really sucks at salsa.

"Would you like me to show you the step again?" I ask tentatively.

He ruffles the back of his head. "Thank you. I'm terrible at this but I want to learn. It's a surprise for my girlfriend: she loves salsa." I smile broadly at the guy. How sweet of him!

"Julio, will you please show this gentleman the basic step again?" Jack says, taking my hand with a fluid movement and positioning himself in front of me. My hands burn at the sudden contact with Jack's hand and bare shoulder. His shoulder muscles are hard beneath my palm, his skin warm and smooth, and I itch to slide my hand down and caress his broad chest. "Ready?" he asks. I bob my head, grinning back at him. He takes a step forward, then one backwards, moving us effortlessly, leading me into the sensuous rhythm. My feet move of their own accord, the memory of the steps surfacing from the back of my mind, and my body naturally falls in tune with Jack's and the music.

"You look gorgeous in this cute little tracksuit," Jack says for my ears only. I fight back a smile and try to keep my breath under control, aware of his bare, glorious upper body just inches away from mine and of the people moving around us. I get a whiff of Jack's cologne and it suddenly takes a huge effort not to get distracted and step on his sexy feet.

"You forgot to tell me that you actually teach this class, Mr. Kendall."

"I didn't forget; I intentionally omitted it."

"Why?"

"I wanted to surprise you."

The song that's playing blends into a new, faster one and Jack stops us. "I want to dance with you later, baby, feel your body move against mine," he whispers in my ear and my breath catches. He holds my gaze for what feels like forever then takes a step back, switching back into teacher-mode.

"All right, folks," he says to the room, "now watch this new position we're gonna learn tonight. It's called hammerlock, or sombrero arm lock."

The rest of the class flies and just when I'm warming up, it's time to wrap up. Pff.

"Well done, everybody. For those of you who want to practice the steps you've learned, we're heading to the Barrio Latino in Gloucester Road in… thirty minutes," Julio says, glancing at his watch. We clap our hands and cheer as we hurry to the showers.

"Hey," Jack says, taking my hand gently, "see you shortly?"

"Yes, Mr. Teacher," I say, sliding into the ladies' changing room.

***

When we arrive, the Barrio Latino is absolutely packed and believe me when I say that although we're in London, the official language in this place is definitely not English. I never knew that so many people went out dancing on a weekday;

then again, I've never really gone out a lot, even when I was with Nico, except to go see him perform.

Nico hates salsa music, which is one reason I gave up dancing in the first place. The other reason is that even though he never wanted to learn how to dance, he would go mad whenever I danced with another guy. I can't deny that my ex's possessiveness excited me and made me feel wanted in a raw kind of way, but Jack has been showing me how he can care about me, and still respect my space. His presence by my side is subtle and yet very powerful, and so irresistible that sometimes I feel like a satellite orbiting around him. Yes, I'm definitely falling for him. Hard.

We step inside and noisy Spanish talking immediately surrounds us. Jack relaxes visibly in the dim light of the club and takes off the teacher's hat. He truly is mesmerizing – face, body and soul   and I can't believe this man wants to be with me. I inhale his clean, manly scent deeply as he leans to me to take my jacket. Every chance is good.

"How are you?" he asks, hugging me tightly. Mmmh, I've been waiting all evening for this.

"Very good," I answer in his chest, lightly trailing my fingertips down the side of his stomach. I smile when I hear his breath catch at my touch. He captures my wandering hand in his and kisses it softly.

"Did you enjoy my class?"

"I loved it."

I step closer because I can't help it: I want to be as close to Jack as a public place allows us to be. He runs a hand through my locks and I sigh in delight. "You worked hard. You deserve something to drink."

"And so do you."

We sit at the bar. While Jack orders our drinks, I retrieve my phone from my pocket and glance at the missed calls showing on my display. Nico has been calling me non-stop for the last half hour; my guess is that he noticed that I wasn't drooling over him in the audience at the pub.

I don't feel like talking to Nico right now. It's loud in here and he'll probably be due back on stage soon anyway. I'm tired of him calling me at all times. He ditches me and then he keeps calling. I really don't understand the guy and right now I'm determined not to waste my time overthinking. I'm trying to go on with my life here. Being out dancing with Jack is all I want to focus on tonight.

I look around, sipping on my drink. Sitting next to Jack, with our thighs brushing, is very distracting but I try to observe the decoration of this place: the Barrio Latino is a fantastic club. I've actually never been in a place like this. It's all wood inside from the bar to the tables to the floor. White ropes hang on the high walls, creating the illusion of a vessel, and blue drapes decorate the ceiling, giving a fresh feeling of moving waves. This place makes you feel like you're sailing in the Caribbean.

"I love this place," I say in Jack's ear.

"So do I. The owners are Puerto Ricans."

"Friends of yours?"

He shrugs, his easy smile curving his lips while he takes a drag of his Cuba Libre.

"You are a very good teacher, you know. I'm impressed."

"And you're a natural," Jack says softly, and all I can think about is how gorgeous this man is. He's wearing a blue button-up shirt that matches his eyes, at the same time creating a delicious contrast with his mocha skin, and my heart beats faster, longing to admire his body from the waist down for the first time. All of a sudden, I wish we were anywhere else, alone.

I sit straighter on my stool. I'm shocked by the physical attraction I feel for Jack. I've never felt this way before for anybody but Nico. This new, intense feeling is so powerful. It makes me feel alive.

"Hey," Julio says, walking up to us, "what's your name again?"

"Lisa."

Julio takes my hand and tugs me towards the dance floor. "She needs to practice," he tells Jack over my shoulder and positions himself in front of me. The music is slow and sweet and Julio takes full advantage of it: he puts his open hand wide on my lower back and presses me to him. I stiffen: he smells of rum and our bodies are far closer than I'm comfortable with, but I can't help but move with him.

"Where are you from?" Julio asks.

"Italy."

"Ah, Italiana!" Then he frowns. "You are blond. You don't look Italian."

I roll my eyes mentally but keep a straight face. After all, although this is not Jack's main job, Julio is his colleague at the gym and I don't want to offend him.

"Mmmh, I like pizza," Julio drawls. He adds more pressure to my lower back, effectively closing the little space I've been keeping between us. I can actually feel him from knee to belly now and it's definitely uncomfortable. I stop abruptly and take a step back, into familiar arms that slide around my waist, detaching me from Julio completely.

"Not like that with her, Julio." Jack's jaw is set above my head and the warning in his voice is clear.

"Hey, sorry, hermano, lo siento," Julio says, looking from Jack to me. "I didn't realize she was with you. You're lucky, she's a natural." He winks at me and shoulders his way towards a group of girls.

"I'm sorry," Jack says, turning me to face him. "Do you wanna go?"

"No, I'm fine. Thanks for rescuing me, though."

"Are you sure?" he asks again, searching my eyes.

"I'm sure. Let's just have a good time."

Jack starts to move and I fall into step with him. "Julio's a bit exuberant sometimes," he says of his friend, but I don't care. All I can think about is Jack. He's a fantastic salsa dancer: he's obviously in his element and the way he moves his hips should be illegal.

"Where did you learn to dance like this?"

"I started to dance in New York, when I was a kid. As I told you, my dad was born in Puerto Rico and was always very proud of his culture. Dancing was as natural as breathing in our community."

I smile, imagining little Jack moving his first, uncertain salsa steps: I bet he broke a few girls' hearts even back then.

"You feel good in my arms," he says, and I melt inside. His words are direct, simple, and sweet, just like him. I like it It makes me want to be closer to him, and not only in a physical way. With one elegant movement, Jack spins me around and when I land clumsily against his hard chest, he holds me there. I smile sheepishly against his shoulder. The music is slower now, sensual, and my body moves forward naturally, as if it belonged against Jack's. The contact with him feels electrifying, still new and yet familiar, and my hands skim over his broad shoulders and wrap behind his neck. Jack's body creates a delicious friction against mine as we move back and forth to match the lazy rhythm. He groans in my ear and bites gently on my earlobe. A shiver runs up my spine and my parted lips find his neck. His flesh tastes so delicious that I want to cry with joy.

Jack stops us abruptly and stares down at me, his gaze so soft and sexy at the same time. He walks me backwards, past the bar, and I don't mind at all: I'm done dancing. He halts in a darker corner and hugs me tight, breathing deeply into my hair. There's no mistaking the attraction he feels for me: I can feel it against my belly and it makes my pulse jump.

"I've been trying to keep my distance but every time I see you, it gets harder and harder to not touch these luscious curves, not to kiss your mouth," he says in a strained voice. "I want you so bad, baby."

"Oh, Jack…"

"Just this once," he says then he leans down and softly touches his lips to mine. A wave of unapologetic desire rages inside me. Jack deepens the kiss and I moan in his warm, demanding mouth. He closes his fists in my locks; his lips are so hungry on mine and so completely manly that my head actually spins. This is, by far, the most intense kiss I've ever given and received.

"Oh my God," I murmur, blinking rapidly, my fingers digging into Jack's shoulders for support.

"Baby, did you feel that?" he says in a gruff voice that makes me tremble all over again.

Oh yes, I did. Words fail me so I just nod. I'm in a total daze.

"From the very first moment I laid eyes on you, I knew there would be sparks between us, but this…you... you are truly amazing, sweetheart," he says in awe.

Can somebody please stop time? I just never want this moment to end.

"Does that mean you're gonna kiss me again?" I ask, a bit out of breath. Jack is intoxicating and I'm definitely under *his* influence right now. "Please," I say, biting my lip. I guess I look and sound like a petulant little girl who's asking for one more cookie right now but that's the thing: now that I know how delicious Jack's kisses are, I just want more of them.

"This is completely unwise but I don't think I can help it right now," he says fiercely against my lips, before covering my mouth with his with the hunger of a starved man. I savor every moment of his long, hot assault, basking in the warmth of his palms moving up my spine from my lower back to my neck and then down again; and when my back arches involuntarily under his skilled touch, he takes a step back. "Let's get out of here," he says between ragged breaths. "We need to talk."

FIFTEEN

I shuffle my wet shoes on the doormat and step into Jack's apartment. "Oh, Jack, this is so cool."

It's more than that: it's luxurious. I knew Jack had a good job, but this? I didn't expect him to live in such a fancy place. Until now I hadn't realized that Jack is well off. I guess his sporty little car should have been a clue but because I don't particularly care about material things, I guess I hadn't connected the dots.

I glance around the spacious living area: his furniture definitely did not come from a big department store, like mine. I skim my finger over the shiny black marble surface of Jack's kitchen island and walk slowly towards the beige leather sofa. An image of my battered green couch pops up in my head and I almost laugh out at the abyssal gap. "Are you rich?"

Jack throws his head back and laughs a belly laugh that does things to my pulse.

"What's so funny?"

"You are."

"Well, you told me I could be open with you so I thought I'd ask you a question."

"That wasn't open, it was blunt."

I gape at him. "No it wasn't!"

He exhales dramatically. "I'm afraid I've created a monster." He walks to his fancy iPod docking station and touches the screen. Soft music starts to play in the background; very nice.

"Well? Are you?" I insist, arching a brow.

"My father is of humble origins. He moved to New York from Puerto Rico when he was a kid and grew up in the Bronx. My mother's family is of noble English heritage, but my great-grandfather was a gambler and squandered almost the entire family fortune on the wrong bets. In other words, my job pays very well," he says, shrugging one shoulder.

"I didn't know that salsa dancing paid so well," I say, smirking.

He shakes his head and grins at me. "What would you like to drink? I have Coke and orange juice," he says, inspecting the inside of his fridge.

"I'm okay, thanks."

He closes the fridge and comes to sit down next to me on the couch. I love how he drapes his arm across my shoulders, as if it is the most natural thing to do. I automatically snuggle closer to him. "How did you get into Harvard?"

"Scholarship. I'm still paying some of my student's debt but that's no longer a financial burden at this stage."

I search his face for smugness or any other sign of arrogance but all I see in this man's beautiful face is neutral pragmatism. I can relate to that so I nod, waiting for him to continue, to ease my insatiable thirst for knowing more about him, but I feel he's done talking about himself for now. "And are you rich?" he asks instead, leaning closer to me, his eyes smiling at me, and I almost lose myself in that deep blue. Wow. Only after a long moment do I manage to find my tongue.

"No, I'm afraid I'm not, but I'm a hard worker," I say, pushing my chin up.

"There you go: that's another thing we have in common."

"And what else do you think we have in common?"

"Well, we are both tasteful exceptions to national-slash-racial stereotypes."

"I guess we are," I say, mirroring his grin. "What else?"

"We both like Japanese food."

"Very true. Anything else?"

Jack's expression sobers and he stares down at me for a long moment. "Both of us have been in a damaging relationship in the past."

I nod at him. Now this totally makes sense. "Do you want to talk about it?" I ask softly, skimming my fingertips over Jack's cheek. His jaw is set and jumps under my touch. This wonderful man is so big and confident, and yet he looks so vulnerable right now, sitting here next to me, that all I want to do is wrap my arms around him and never let him go.

Jack never intended to speak about his previous

relationship and he is considering ending this conversation before it even starts: it's written all over his face. Then he sighs deeply. "I just want you to know that this is not about you. I mean, my trust issues have nothing to do with you personally," he says cautiously, and I nod, hoping he will open up to me, because right now, this no longer has anything to do with curiosity; it's simply the most important thing in the world for me. Please, Jack, let me in, please, please, please...

"My ex..." My chest contracts at his pained expression.

I squeeze his hand. How can any woman, anybody, mistreat Jack? I swallow hard. "How did she hurt you?"

Jack shakes his head. "I'm a simple guy, you know. I don't idealize people and I'm not looking for a perfect woman. I just want to find a good girl to share my life with, somebody who will stand by my side, who wants to have a family with me one day."

I know this will sound crazy   I've known the guy just for a few weeks, for God's sake   but right in this moment, I want to be that girl. I want to be at Jack's side for a long, long time. "It sounds like your ex couldn't be that girl for you," I say, trying to keep my overwhelming emotions at bay. This is about Jack now.

"I can take anything, but there is one thing I will not compromise on."

"And what is that?" I ask, holding my breath. I don't know why, and this is completely irrational, but I feel that my life is never going to be the same after this man shares this part of him with me.

Jack turns to me and looks so deep into my eyes that I feel his blue gaze reach out to touch my soul. "Honesty."

"Honesty," I repeat.

He nods.

"This is why I don't want to rush things between us, while you're still working things out with your ex. I care about you too much." He takes my hands in his and looks at them. "You don't even realize how much power you hold in these little hands of yours."

Oh my God, is Jack worried that I could hurt him? But

how could I ever?

"Jack, Nico and I are finished. We broke up months ago, and he's been seeing other women." *Well, Lisa, that didn't stop you from sleeping with him, did it?* the most sincere part of me admits, but it's just a distant voice in my head and I easily silence it.

"He's still chasing after you, Lisa. I know how a man's head works and from what I've seen, he's far from finished with you."

Is he? An unwanted rush of excitement pushes through my system and blends with guilt. Oh God, here I am, sitting with Jack, hanging on his every word after he kissed me senseless at the club, and the best I can do is get hot and bothered because he suggested that my ex may still be interested in me?

I don't know how I manage to keep a poker face but I do. I'll elaborate later, I tell myself. "That's only in his head, Jack; I'm working hard to make sure my story with Nico stays in the past." And that is a hundred and fifty percent true. In my own random way, I am trying to write the final chapter of my story with Nico.

"I do believe that you're trying, but this is not only about you, Lisa. I just have a feeling he won't give you up easily."

I rub my forehead. I don't want to talk about Nico, especially with Jack: it makes me utterly uncomfortable. "Why does it matter? Nico and I are no longer together and I actually doubt that he has ever loved me." I stifle a sob. There's a thick blend of hollow and hope that's choking me right now, but somehow I manage to finish my thought. "I didn't think this could be possible, but since you came into my life, day by day, you've been pushing Nico out of my head. That's how wonderful you are."

Oh, did I just say that aloud? I guess I did, because something incredibly powerful flickers in Jack's eyes. I can see that he's trying to process my words, which sound audacious even to my own ears. I may not be completely there yet, I tell myself, but I mean them, and that's what really matters, isn't it?

"I bet he's still calling you."

"I don't always pick up or call him back."

Jack stares at me for a long moment. "I don't like to share," he says in a low, firm voice. "I want to be absolutely clear on this. Do you understand?"

I nod, completely mesmerized by his intense gaze.

"Do you, baby?"

"I do."

He cups my cheek and skims his thumb over it gently. "You are an incredible woman, Lisa. I don't need to go all the way with you to claim you as mine, although God knows that I can't stop thinking about how your sexy little body would feel beneath me." The pad of his thumb brushes my bottom lip and I lick it. Jack's breath catches and he moves his hand to the back of my head. "I'm gonna take it slow with you, for your own sake as well as for mine. But I can promise you one thing: by the time I make love to you, your ex will only be a distant memory, and I'll personally make sure that he stays right at the back of your mind, where he belongs."

Whoa. I shiver at the combination of Jack's fierce expression and gentle touch, at his sweetness and determination. His words wrap around my heart and tears sting at the corner of my eyes. Is Jack the counter spell I've been waiting for, after all?

He leans closer, searching my face. "There's something about you that makes me want to -" He blinks and shakes his head.

"To do what, Jack?" I whisper.

"You're amazing, inside and out."

My eyes moist. That is such a wonderful thing to say. I wipe my tears with the back of my hand and when Jack takes me into his arms and sits me on his lap, I go willingly. "Thanks, Jack."

"For what, babe?"

I shrug one shoulder. "For wanting to be around me, I guess."

Jack smiles tenderly. He kisses the top of my head and I make myself comfortable against his chest. He groans in my ear and kisses my neck.

"You feel so good, so soft and warm."

He kisses me slowly this time, his passion firmly in check. What would it take, I wonder, for me to make Jack's self-control finally snap? I shift in his lap, and I stifle a gasp at the delicious feel of his hardness underneath me.

"We'll take it step by step, and when you are finally in my bed, I will make it so good for you, over and over again, that you won't remember your name."

I smile sheepishly at this American man, at his promise that takes my breath away. Maybe he's slowly stealing my heart.

Minnie Riperton's soft voice fills Jack's living room. Oh, I love this song. *Lovin' you is easy 'cause you're beautiful, making love with you is all I wanna do…* I close my eyes and hum with the music.

"Would you like to dance this one, baby?"

Oh, my God, yes! I shriek in my head. I bit my lower lip and nod. We sway at the sweet rhythm and I can't take my eyes or my hands off Jack. God, this man in my arms has some seriously sexy moves. Right now I wish he was less considerate and much, much more reckless. But then it wouldn't be Jack, and I wouldn't change a thing about him.

I let my forehead drop against his neck and inhale his delicious scent deeply. Mmmh, I feel like I'm floating on a cloud. "You know, you actually made my head spin earlier in the club; I mean, like, physically spin," I say, sheepishly.

He chuckles. "So did you."

"Did I really?"

"Oh yes, you did, baby," he says, locking his eyes with mine. "Never underestimate the effect you have on me."

"When did I make your head spin?"

"When you kissed my neck at the club."

"Like this?" I ask, nibbling Jack's neck just under his earlobe.

His arms tighten around me. "You're gonna make my life a misery until you're finally completely mine, aren't you?" he says, squeezing my hips.

No one else can make me feel the colors that you bring, I sing softly in Jack's ear. His face splits in two with a grin. You know when the sky opens after a spring squall and the sun comes out, warm and blinding? That's exactly how I feel right now, as I wrap my arms firmly around Jack's neck to make sure this man is real.

SIXTEEN

"Well, your boyfriend must be head over heels for you, Ms. Castelli," Mr. Conrad says, adjusting his thick glasses over his nose. I turn a darker shade of pink then my boss smiles indulgently and disappears into his office.

"They are beautiful," Sarah says in awe.

I look down at the lovely bouquet sitting on my desk, my heart pumping fast in my chest. "He's very thoughtful," I say. I usually don't talk about my private life with my colleagues but I feel I can trust Sarah so the other day I admitted to her that the reason for the goofy smile that has taken permanent residence on my face is a guy. Well, she had already guessed that, anyway.

"Thoughtful? That's what you call three dozen red roses? The guy has it bad, my dear! And he wants you," Sarah says, chuckling softly. "Aren't you going to read the card?" she asks, pointing to the white little envelope I'm clutching in my hand.

I hate to admit it, but doubts are creeping on me. The flowers *must* be from Jack: Nico wouldn't do something like this for me, right? He never sent me flowers while we were together, so why would he do it now? Still…

I open the card with trembling hands and sigh with relief.

Happy two months anniversary, baby. Lunch together? Miss you, J.

Oh! Jack and I have been seeing each other for two months already? I hadn't realized.

How fast time flies when you're happy. And I am happy, I repeat in my head, a huge grin spreading on my face. I can barely believe that only two months ago I couldn't see myself moving on from Nico, and today not only have I another man in my life, but he makes me *happy*. I move the crystal vase with the flowers to the side of my desk, so that I can access my laptop and go back to work. It's either now or never.

"How romantic of him… What's his name?" Sarah asks. We've grown closer over the last weeks and I feel I'm ready to tell her who's been making my heart beat fast.

"His name's Jack."

"So sweet! You know, Mike used to send me flowers when we were dating," Sarah says, dreamingly. "That was before Molly came along and we got married." She puts a delicate hand on my arm. "Just don't forget this moment, how exciting this is. When you get married and have children, romance just flies out the window."

My heart expands with hope at the thought of a future with Jack and I blink in shock. Could Jack and I grow old together? Could he be the One?

I boot my laptop and fish my phone out of my bag. How much will I be able to get done this morning? Hopefully, Mr. Conrad will forgive my scarce productivity today: it's my anniversary, after all.

***

Jack and I step out of Dino's and into the sun. I stretch in contentment at his side. He takes my hand and kisses it. I love it when he intertwines his fingers with mine and holds my hand securely in his.

"What a lovely day. Just a few more degrees and I wouldn't need a jacket."

"You're always cold. How's that even possible with all that hot, Mediterranean blood flowing in your veins?"

I make a face and he chuckles. "And you're always hot," I say, suggestively, skimming my gaze over him lazily. Jack does always look good, but in his charcoal dress suit and blue tie that matches his eyes? Well, he looks like a god fallen from above.

"Are you ogling me, baby?"

"Maybe I am," I answer sweetly. "What are you gonna do about it?"

Raw desire flickers in his eyes locked on my lips, and everything around me fades away: the shy warmth of the sun, the people walking in all directions around us, the clapping and cheering coming from somewhere on the other side of the square.

"You know, one of these days I'm gonna dive into that

blue and never come back," I whisper, skimming my fingertips over Jack's temple. "If you need me, you're gonna find me there, deep in the blue."

Jack's grip on me tightens. "You're lucky that we're in public," he whispers back, "or I'd just kiss you senseless."

"I wish."

Jack stifles a groan and captures my lips in an intense, far-too-short kiss. Then he takes a step back. "Come on, baby. I have a meeting in thirty-five minutes."

I roll my eyes mockingly but I actually love Jack's dedication to his job.

We cross the square to where a large number of people has gathered, which happens to be in front of my office. "What's going on?" I think aloud. Jack is taller, maybe he can see through the human wall.

When the first few notes of a guitar drift in the air, I stop dead in my tracks. I know that song. Nico composed it after the first night we spent together. "What the hell is he doing here?" I say under my breath.

"It's your ex," Jack says, flatly. I gaze up at him: he's staring right ahead, over most people's heads, and if a look could kill, Nico would be in ashes right now.

"Let me see," I say, shouldering my way to the front of the group as politely as I can: and there stands Nico, playing and singing away as if he didn't have a care in the world. When he sees me, he locks his eyes with mine and smirks. Damn it! Why can't he just leave me alone?

By the time he plays the last note of his song and thanks his audience, I can barely contain my anger. I'm so going to give him a piece of mind, I think to myself, crossing my arms over my chest.

With all the time in the world, Nico puts his guitar down and swaggers up to me. "Ciao, amore."

"Don't call me love," I hiss.

He shoves his hands deep into his pockets. "It's not over between us, love. You need to recognize it."

A flame of rage ignites in my chest. I'm so done with Nico's manipulations and intrusions in my life. I inhale deeply:

I'm just about to explode here, in the middle of the square, and nothing – not pride, or the crowd around us, or even Jack, standing just a few feet away with his eyes firmly trailed on me – absolutely nothing will stop me now. "Nicolas, are you for real? You left me!" I yell in Italian. "You are such an idiot! Just leave me alone!"

Nico braces his hands on his narrow hips and looks down at me. "Elisabetta, you may want it or not, but it is not over between us," he says, loud and clear in English, and I'm one hundred percent positive that that's for Jack's sake; and that's just the last straw.

It's my turn to brace my hands on my hips. If Jack heard what my ex said, as I'm sure he did, he also needs to hear what I'm making of it. "Go to hell, Nico!" I yell in English. And what do you think Nico does? Cringe? Apologize? Just finally leave me alone? Of course not! He throws his head back and laughs.

"You're such a spitfire, love, in public *and* in private," he says, looking over my head.

I turn to follow his gaze; Jack is standing right behind me, hands in his pockets, his head tilted to one side. I shiver at the coldness of his stare. Thank God it's not for me: I don't ever want to be at the receiving end of that stare. As if he is pulled in by my gaze, Jack steps to my side. "Are you all right, baby?"

"Yes," I mumble, unconvinced. I feel small and more than a bit intimidated sandwiched between these two men, surrounded by the tension that oozes from their big bodies. Jack's eyes level to Nico's again.

"The only reason why I don't kick your sorry ass right here in front of an audience is that Lisa can step up for herself, and I respect her too damn much for that. But don't you think that I'm not watching you: I am, and I don't like what I'm seeing."

Nico's smile fades and Jack's voice goes down another octave. "If you make a claim on her one more time, if you cause her just another ounce of pain, if I see her drop just one more tear for you, I swear to God that I'll personally deal with you and you'll be sorry for a long, long time."

I stare up at Jack in a mix of shock and awe. "Let's go,

baby." He takes my arm and gently stirs me towards the GBG building.

"What are you looking at? Move over!" I hear Nico yelling angrily behind us. People don't often see a scene like this here, I guess: it took two Italians, one American, and a ton of pent-up frustration to shake things up in London's stiff financial district. My cheeks flame: I hope nobody from the office was passing by or looking out of the window. *Fat chance, Lisa: it's lunchtime and you're 20 feet from your office's reception.*

"Lisa." I look up at Jack. His eyes are soft as they search my face. "Don't be embarrassed. This is not your fault." It isn't? I wonder to myself. Maybe I should have been firmer with Nico, given a clear cut to the past, but I just don't know what to do with all the history we have together. Should I just throw it behind me and move on, as if I'd never met my ex? Should I try to be friends with him? Is it even possible to be friends with a former boyfriend? Damn, I just don't know. And it really drives me mad that after being my first everything that a man can ever be to a woman, Nico is also my first ex. Argh!

"He makes me so angry at times that I want to strangle him!" I hiss, stomping my foot in my office lobby, my high heels clicking on the shiny tiled floor. Heather arches her brows from behind the reception desk and glances down again. First Jack's flowers this morning, then this scene with Nico: by now she must think that my life outside the office is a lot of fun and must be wondering how she'd never noticed before.

Jack closes his hands around my fists. His touch is soothing and I feel some of the tension leave my shoulders.

"Don't let him get to you, Lisa."

I take a big breath in, then out. "I know that you're right. It's just that… well, at least I've proven to you where Nico and I stand now. Hopefully I've reassured you that there's nothing between me and Nico and we can just move on. There must be a silver lining in this messy afternoon, after all," I say, snorting.

Jack just stares at me, his face sober and unreadable. Where's the smile I thought would come? My pulse accelerates instantly. "Jack, say something, please."

"Not here," he says, glancing around the lobby. Sure enough Heather is looking at us sideways, pretending that she's typing.

"Let's go in there," I say, pointing to a private waiting room. I close the door behind us and lock it. "Jack, I'm so sorry that Nico ruined our lunch."

"Don't apologize, baby, there's no need to."

"He's so infuriating! He has this gift of bringing the worst out in me! I rarely indulge in violent thoughts, but by God, I swear that for a moment, I contemplated hitting him out there! Can you see now how it's over between Nico and me?"

Jack looks at me for a long moment then says, "What I see is the power he still has on you, baby."

I blink. "What? What do you mean?"

"Lisa, he wants your attention, whenever he feels he needs it. If you ignore him, he provokes you until he gets it. Anger is just one of the feelings he aims to arouse in you, probably not his first choice if you ask me, but it obviously works."

He's right, Lisa. You know he's right.

I drop on a chair, pressing the heels of my hands to my eyes. I thought I'd shown Jack that I'm over Nico, while apparently Nico has just managed to show Jack just how much control he still holds on my emotions. On top of that, I've just made a fool of myself in public and fostered at least one month of gossip in the office. Good job, Lisa!

"What's the opposite of love?"

"Hate," I reply automatically.

Jack shakes his head. "Indifference."

I cast my glance down, holding back tears of anger. Jack opens his arms and I slide onto his lap. Relief washes over me when he closes his arms around me. "This is gonna be a rocky ride, baby. You've got to keep strong," he whispers in my ear. I look up into Jack's eyes: they're so soft and caring and understanding. I touch my lips to his: I need to feel him on my lips. He opens to the kiss and slides his tongue into my mouth, his hand skimming up over my back and cupping the back of my neck possessively. White hot desire dances a crazy dance in my belly and I mentally thank Nancy for the hundredth time for putting Jack's name down on the heart-shaped card.

"I'd better go, baby, if you don't want to finish this on the table," Jack says hoarsely. Mmmh, I'd better see this American boy to the door right now or I'll never go back up to my desk again. "I'll call you later," he says, stamping a kiss on my lips. "I can't wait to taste those plump lips of yours again," he whispers, before slipping thorough the revolving doors of the GBG building.

I ignore Heather's curious glances and take the elevator up to my floor. By the time it chimes, I've pushed my hair away from my face and squared my shoulders. I walk briskly to my desk, just in case anybody who witnessed my little show earlier has the bad idea to ask any questions. But I know I won't be able to avoid Sarah: I'm meeting with her in fifteen minutes to discuss the progress of the summer party. Hopefully she'll have mercy and go easy on me.

Sarah walks up to my desk right on time and beams down at me. I collect my files and trail after her towards our meeting room. She stops at the door and turns. "Unless you want to talk about this, which I really doubt you do, there's just two things that I'm gonna say about what I saw and heard downstairs."

I nod warily.

"Number one, follow your heart, it knows what's right for you."

Does it?

"Number two: either guy you choose, you're one lucky girl!"

Sarah chuckles at the face I make and, good to her word, bless her, she spares me any other comment on my love life.

I drag myself through the rest of the afternoon. God, this day has completely drained me emotionally. Five long hours later, I finally walk into my room. I drop my handbag on the floor and collapse on my bed. I'm exhausted. Thank God Penny is not at home yet: I wouldn't even know where to start to tell her about the square incident. It's just too disturbing.

A short nap is just what I need, I tell myself as my eyelids drift closed…

***

I wake up in the darkness of my room and stretch lazily on my bed. What time is it? I smell the rich scent of coffee and my stomach growls loudly: it's time to have dinner. I slide out of bed and realize that I fell asleep in my, now- wrinkled, work clothes. I drop them in my laundry basket and quickly change into a t-shirt and tracksuit bottoms. I open the door of my room and hear Penny's voice speaking in Spanish. Since she moved in with me over a year ago, I've been picking up her language effortlessly: it's easy enough for an Italian to understand Spanish if it is spoken slowly.

"I said I'm not gonna go to that wedding with you. You're wasting your time."

I stop in my tracks. I know I shouldn't eavesdrop, but I can't help myself.

"Just promise me you'll think about it. You don't need to decide now," a deep male voice says. "It's just for a couple of days. You were friends with her too, after all."

"Yes, I was, but all of a sudden we no longer were such good friends, thanks to you," Penny says, pointedly.

"Penelope, why can't you just forget and move on? How much longer are you going to punish me? Can't you see that I'm dying here?"

Punish him? For what?

"Finish your coffee, I need to study tonight. I've got another exam coming up soon."

I square my shoulders and tiptoe into the kitchen. Penny is leaning against our big fridge, arms crossed over her chest. There's a guy standing in front of her, and…

Oh, my God!

"Paco?" I ask in astonishment. "What are you doing here?"

Penny's face swings to mine and her features relax immediately. "Madre de Dios, Chica, I thought you were lying dead in your bed! You've been out for over two hours!"

I arch a brow: I will not be sidetracked. "Penny, what's

138

Paco doing in our kitchen?" I ask, pointing my finger to the guy, who's shaking his head.

Penny exhales heavily. "This is Miguel, Paco's twin."

"Oh, the photographer?"

"Did you talk about me with your friend?" Miguel asks, his eyes widening with hope.

"Absolutely not," she answers. He cringes and smiles sadly at me. Wow. This guy is as handsome as his model twin brother: same flawless face, lean body, and chocolate eyes.

"You must be Lisa," Miguel says, extending his hand, and I take it. "My brother told me about you."

"He did?" I ask in surprise. Did Paco tell his brother that I eat like a pig?

"Oh yes. You've made an impression. Not many women have turned him down. Make none, before you."

I blush. If they only knew that I ended up spending the night with Nico... some things are so much better left unsaid. "So Penny, are you going to a wedding?" I ask, eager for a subject change.

"No!" Penny says at the same time that Miguel says "Yes." She glares at him. What did he do to her? Mmmh, thinking about it, I might not want to be in their crossfire.

"She doesn't wanna go with me," Miguel says. "She's as stubborn as a mule sometimes." I look in astonishment at this man who's not afraid of Penny's wrath. I have to say though that there isn't an ounce of accusation in his tone. All I can hear is... adoration?

"Cut it, Miguel. I'm not gonna go with you. God knows what ideas that'd put in that thick head of yours. Now, if you'll excuse me, I'm going to take that," Penny says, snatching up her ringing phone from the couch and slamming her bedroom door behind her.

I look at Penny's friend sideways. He's staring at the floor between his legs. This is rather awkward, me and Miguel standing in the kitchen in uncomfortable silence. I open the fridge and take out tomatoes and cheese. "Would you like a sandwich?"

"I've been in love with her since we were sixteen," he says, just like that, out of the blue. "She was already beautiful at that age. And smart   the smartest in our class. She loved to study. You could already see back then that she would have a smooth academic path and a successful career. I kept chasing her with the excuse that I wanted to photograph her. I wanted to capture her huge fawn eyes, her Mona Lisa smile, and that mane of black hair that she would always wear down. But she wasn't interested in wasting time with any of us idiots in her school, obviously. You know how dumb teenage boys can be. I played that game too, because I needed to feel accepted by my friends. I may be the spit image of my brother but I've never been as self-assured as he is. It's not by chance that he earns his living in front of the camera while I hide behind it. So that's what I did, I secretly admired her from afar."

Oh, this is fascinating. Penny once told me about falling in love very young, but she never elaborated. Was Miguel her first love? I push the ingredients for my sandwich across the counter and sit down at the kitchen table, motioning Miguel to do the same. His big body drops on to a chair with a sigh and I wait patiently for him to continue. After a long moment, he speaks again.

"This girl who's getting married, Maria, she was in our class, too. She was Penny's best friend. One day they had a fight, and Maria yelled that she'd seen Penny groping me behind the school wall. That was so absurd, of course, although God knows it that was one of my favorite fantasies," he says, sheepishly. Then his expression sobers. "Anyway, instead of clearing Penny's thrashed reputation, I played the cool, good-looking teenager, or so I thought. I didn't say a word to help her, even when Maria came out clean. I don't know why: maybe I just hoped that Penny would eventually give in and be with me. Everybody thought there had been something between us anyway at that stage. I should've known better. Penny never forgave me for becoming the target of so much gossip. And she just can't let it go. She says it's not for the harm my silence caused in itself but because I was a coward. To this day, she still doesn't believe that a stupid boy can grow into a devoted and loving husband."

Husband? "Husband? You asked Penny to marry you?" I ask in astonishment.

"I do every six months. I still love her, you know, witchery stuff and all. In fact, I was the first victim of her witchcraft."

"You were? What spell did she do on you?"

He smiles sadly. "A love spell, or so she said. And I complied eagerly. Too bad it didn't work both ways."

Penny storms back into the kitchen and drops her phone on the table with a loud thud. "I'll go to this stupid wedding with you on one condition," she says, holding up her index finger.

"Ask for anything," Miguel says, hopefully.

"Our friend is having a baby in the summer. I want you to take the most amazing pictures of Monique, Andy, and their baby. I want them to be breath-taking pictures: better than those ones you take for the *National Geographic*."

"It'll be my pleasure to do that, my love."

"Good," she says with a sharp nod then she turns to me. "Baby's present sorted."

"I'm gonna be going," Miguel says, standing up. He's beaming like a child on Christmas morning. He's obviously got what he came for. Fair play to him: Penny is a tough nut to crack. "I'll pick you up on Wednesday morning, love. We're gonna catch the 11.15am flight out to Madrid."

"Send me the details by email. I need to buy my ticket."

"I already bought your ticket."

Penny's eyes narrow. "So sure of yourself, aren't you, Miguel Lopez?"

He shrugs a shoulder. "I like to take risks."

Penny shows him to the door. *Stop kissing me everywhere!* I hear her protest, and I chuckle under my breath. After what I've just witnessed, I think I'll stop thinking about matchmaking my roommate and Lallo, after all.

She walks back into the kitchen.

"So?" I ask, finally taking a long over-due first bite of my sandwich.

"So, there's nothing to say."

"Penny! The guy asks you to marry him twice a year and

you call that *nothing*? And why haven't you ever told me about this guy?"

"Because there's nothing to say."

"Ah, come on! Don't tell me that you're still holding a grudge for what happened when you were sixteen."

"He told you?" she asks, her eyes wide.

I nod.

"Of course I don't. That was ten years ago."

"But that's what Miguel thinks."

"I know."

"What's your deal then?"

Penny sits on the chair in front of me and pushes her black shiny locks away from her face. "He's just too much for me: too good-looking, too sweet, and too talented."

"Oh my God, Penny!" I all but yell in astonishment. "Are you serious?"

"I'm dead serious, Lisa. He keeps up with my tantrums and with my silly hobby. Did he tell you that he was my first guinea pig back in the days, one week after I bought my first book about magic? What guy does that?"

"One who's head over heels in love with you?"

Penny covers her eyes with her hands and blushes. I look at what is visible of her face in disbelief: I've never seen her blush before. "He seems like a very decent guy. Do you like him?"

"God, Chica, what's not to like? He's perfect. That's the problem."

It's my time to narrow my eyes. "That's a *problem* in your mind, Penny?"

"You don't understand."

"Oh but I do understand. You're scared to death, amiga mia," I say, smiling smugly.

"I'm not scared!" she says, outraged.

"You are. You're scared of riding that wave, of letting yourself love him. You're scared of being happy next to a man that other women may desire."

"I'm not!"

"But Penny, you're extraordinary, intelligent, and beautiful. You're witty and you're one of the strongest women I know; if

142

you can't handle Miguel Lopez, who can?"

My friend's eyes mist. "Thank you," she whispers. We lock into a long, tight hug. It feels great to be there for her.

"Here," I say, handing her a paper napkin.

"How did your day go?" she asks, sniffing.

Memories of my day come back to me and I'm not sure I want to talk about it. "I think we've had far too much emotional action for one day. What do you say if we just vegetate on our good old couch until sleep claims us?"

"Deal," Penny says without protesting, for once, and I sigh in relief.

SEVENTEEN

I spill hot water from the kettle all over the kitchenette's counter and beat on my lower lip. "God, I'm so nervous," I mutter under my breath, taking a few napkins and wiping up the mess.

"What's wrong with you? You haven't been yourself all day," Sarah asks. She's stirring her tea, watching me under her lashes.

"Tonight after work I'm meeting Jack's friends for the first time."

"Oh, you're due for the friends' test," she says, smiling knowingly.

I roll my eyes dramatically. "Thanks, Sarah, I feel much better now."

"But Lisa, this is a very good sign and very much part of the game. When a man selects women throughout his life, only a few make it to the 'meet my friends' stage. After that, it's only a question of meeting his family before you walk down the aisle. Ta ta ta taa!"

I shake my head and throw the wet napkins into the trash. "I know I shouldn't be so tense but… I'm just…"

"Worried as hell that you'll make a fool of yourself? That his friends will hate you on the spot? That you will embarrass him?"

I look at Sarah in surprise. "How did you guess?"

"Every woman has been there, honey," she says, pouring herself another cup of tea. Yes, English people really like their tea. I put my almost-empty cup down in the sink. I've spilled most of the water on the counter anyway and my stomach is in knots.

"When I first met Mike's friends, Ireland was playing Scotland. We'd gathered in a pub to watch the game. Mike's from Edinburgh, you know, and he expected me to support Scotland. Ha! When I stepped into the club waving an Irish flag, his jaw dropped. His friends still tease him to this day. They're tough on each other, those Scots, but in reality they're just a bunch of grumpy teddy bears," she says, giggling.

"I didn't know you were Irish."

"I was born in London but my dad's originally from Cork, in the south of Ireland. He's the one I get my love for sports from."

"I don't think I'll step into Jack's apartment waving an Italian flag any time soon," I say, rubbing my forehead. "I just don't know what to expect. What if they don't like me, if we just don't click?"

"If they're good friends of Jack's, they will study you but also accept you with open arms at the same time," Sarah says, leaning against the counter. "Your boyfriend obviously wants you in his life. That's all that matters."

My boyfriend. Jack is *my boyfriend*. I still can't believe it. We haven't made love yet, but that's because he wants to give me time to distance myself from my past with Nico. Although he's driving me crazy with want, I understand where he's coming from. We don't need to sleep together, be official, or promise each other 'forever' to be together. The way he's handling this situation, with Nico's frequent attempts to contact me, says a lot about his integrity and only increases my respect for him. Jack is so much more than my boyfriend: he's the best man I know.

Mr. Conrad walks into the kitchenette. He stops right in front of Sarah and me and rubs his chin. "Buongiorno, Signorina Castelli," he says at length.

"Very good, Mr. Conrad!" I say, surprised. Considering his ineptitude for languages, even a super simple sentence like this is a great achievement.

He adjusts his thick glasses and chuckles. "I'm so bad at this. You've got the patience of a saint, Lisa." I smile behind the rim of my cup while Mr. Conrad washes his cup in the sink, puts it to dry, and walks away. I admire that my boss is so hands-on and down to earth. I like those traits in people in general and particularly in leaders. I don't know what I'd do if I suddenly didn't have this job anymore.

"I like working with Mr. Conrad. Hopefully, I'll have the pleasure of doing so for some more time."

Sarah leans to me and says, "If you're worried about the reorg, don't be. Tony from Human Resources told me that GBG's not going to lay anybody off, here in the headquarters or anywhere else in the world. Just don't tell anybody that I told you," she whispers.

I sigh in relief. I really hope this gossip is accurate and I'll soon have one thing less to worry about. If I could just get Nico to stop calling me every thirty minutes, that would help. I'm tempted to let his call go into voicemail but I just don't want to risk him calling me later when I'm with Jack.

"Excuse me for just a moment, Sarah." I retrieve my smartphone from my pocket and touch the green square on my screen. "Nico, will you just stop calling?" I hiss into the phone.

"Hello to you, too, amore."

I turn from Sarah's perplexing stare. There's so much I can handle at once. "Nico, please. You know I'm at work. I can't speak now."

"I need to talk to you."

"No, you don't."

"Come to my place tonight."

I stifle a nervous laugh that sounds creepy even to my own ears. "You can't be serious."

"But I am. Let's order pizza and chat on the couch."

"No."

"Please."

"I said no."

For a few moments I think that Nico has hung up on me.

"Is he better than me in bed?"

"What?" I ask in shock.

"Is he, Lisa?"

"Nico!" I say, struggling to keep my voice low, "what are you? Sixteen?"

"You haven't answered my question."

"And I won't! I can't believe I'm having this conversation with you. I have to go."

"Don't be difficult."

"You're impossible!" I hang up, take a steadying breath,

and turn to face Sarah. She's staring at me, lips pursed in a thin line. "I'm Sorry, Sarah, but I really don't want to talk about this."

"Do you mind if I give you a piece of advice for tonight?"

My heart is pumping fast and I don't know any more if I'm back into panic mode for tonight or if it's the effect of Nico's call. Why does talking to him have to bother me so much? "Go ahead."

"Be yourself around Jack's friends, Lisa, and you'll see. How much you care about him will just shine through, and his friends will love you for that."

I nod, praying silently that my colleague is right.

***

I spot Jack among the crowd and all but jog to him in my heels. He wraps his arms around my waist and leans down to kiss me. Mmmh. Have I said how much I love that he's so affectionate?

"I may get used to your sweet hellos, Mr. Kendall."

"You should," he says, brushing the sensitive spot underneath my ear, and I shiver in delight.

Jack's looking dashing in his black suit and red tie. I wish we weren't on the platform of a busy underground station. My desire for him grows every time I see him, with every gentle touch and passionate kiss, and I don't know how much longer I will be able to hold back. One of these days I may just throw what's left of my patience out the window and drag him to bed.

"Are you thinking what I'm thinking?" he whispers against my parted lips, and I blush.

"Maybe," I say, coyly. Jack flashes his most charming smile; then he sobers up. "Soon," he says, and his voice is so tender and fierce at the same time that I melt right here and now at Bank subway station.

We get on the train and off at Balham, a neighborhood in south-west London. I glance around. I don't know this part of the city but it's beautiful, with its little independent shops and bistros. London can be breath-taking at night.

"Do you fancy a burger?"

"Aren't we meeting with your friends tonight?"

"I told them we would join them later. I wanted to have you all for me for a while first."

I smile back at my boyfriend. How does he always know what to say to make me feel special? "But, a burger? Really? That's so American of you."

"Are you saying that I'm cliché, pizza girl?"

I bite back a laugh and don't resist when Jack tugs me gently towards the traffic light. Rain takes us by surprise and as soon as the green light flashes, we run to the shelter of an old book store on the other side of the street, laughing like teenagers.

Jack takes my wet face into his big, warm hands and kisses me softly. He smells of his spicy cologne, of rain, and man. I grip the front of his jacket tightly. "Did you want to have dinner alone with me too?" he asks against my lips. I capture them with mine in a searing kiss, then flick my tongue across his swollen bottom lip and he groans.

"Yes," I say, breathlessly. "You know how much I long to be alone with you."

He stares down at my lips and shakes his head. "You are driving me completely crazy, baby. I can't sleep. Every time I close my eyes, I see you right there, sprawled on my bed, waiting for me." He closes his mouth on mine again and more sensations burst inside me, set alive by his hot words and mouth and tongue. I want to remember this moment: the soothing sound of rain falling heavily so close to us, the smell of rain and Jack, the damp freshness of this wet evening, Jack's warm hands and mouth on me, and the butterflies dancing in my belly.

Jack suddenly pulls back and stares down at me for a long moment with such hunger and fierceness in his eyes that my breath catches. "Come with me to Oxford on Friday."

"But you said you'd be away this weekend," I say, surprised.

"I'm visiting my mother. I want you to meet her."

Oh, my God! I look at Jack in wonder and shock. Does he really mean it? "You want me to meet your mum?"

He nods. "I want you to see where I spent my summers as a kid, while a little Italian girl was wreaking havoc in the Tuscan valleys," he says, touching my nose with his fingertip. "Will you come with me?"

"Oh, Jack, of course I'll go with you!" I say, burying my face in his neck because he smells so incredible, but especially to hide the tears of joy that are just about to fall.

***

I let myself into my flat, shrug out of my wet jacket and kick my heels off, sighing in relief. I'm beyond exhausted, but the kick of adrenaline of meeting Jack's friends tonight is keeping my blood running quickly. I know I won't be able to fall asleep just yet even if I go to bed now.

I walk into the kitchen and find Penny with her head buried in one of her thick books. She glances up at me. "I was just about to make some more tea."

"I'll do it," I say, picking up her mug from the table. "Long night?"

"Yeah," she says, stretching her arms above her head.

"I don't know how you do this, you know. Working and studying at the same time must be exhausting."

She shrugs one shoulder. "I have no choice at this stage. I'm almost finished."

"Fair play to you, Chica." My hand holding the kettle stops mid-air. The sweetest, saddest melody I've ever heard is drifting in the kitchen from Penny's room, where she keeps her iPod. A husky male voice sings of unrequited love and a broken heart, and my heart stutters. I know that voice.

"What's this song?"

"It's amazing, isn't it? I stopped by at the studio just as Lallo was recording it the other day. I didn't know he could play the piano. Bruce uploaded a copy of that song onto my iPod because I said I loved it."

I busy myself with pouring two cups of tea and sit down in

front of Penny. Lallo composes more music than lyrics, and when he does put down words, he never sings them: that's Nico's job. Lallo's voice is deep and anguished and I shiver at the thought that he decided to sing of his tormented love himself; and that he's singing about me. Thinking that I'm causing my friend pain makes my stomach churn. After he told me how he feels about me, Lallo and I have never touched that subject again. I figured he would feel uncomfortable and I can't deny I would, too. But hearing his thoughts in music now is making me realize that there's so much left unsaid. Maybe we should talk.

"Lisa to Earth."

"Sorry."

Penny tears a pack of cookies open and pushes it between us after taking one. "I miss those Italian almond cookies you always bring back. When are you going back home next?" she asks, munching.

"Not anytime soon, but I can ask Lallo to bring back a few packs. He's going to Milan on Thursday."

"Good girl. I'll also be away this weekend."

"Oh, yeah, you're going to a wedding with a devilishly handsome man who adores you, right? What an effort, Chica."

Penny makes a face.

"Won't you even try to have fun? At least you'll be in your hometown."

"Yeah, my mama and abuela have already started to cook for me. Between the food at the reception and the homemade stuff my family will shove down our throats, I'll probably explode."

"Miguel will have what you don't want. The guy would do anything to please you."

"Ah, stop!" She bites on another cookie and sighs. "I don't know, I have a strange feeling about this weekend. I'd rather stay here with you."

"But I won't be here," I say smugly.

"Where are you going?"

"Jack invited me to go to Oxford with him. He wants me to meet his mum and see all the places where he grew up."

"Oh! But this is great, Lisa! How do you feel about it?"

"Very excited," I say, grinning.

"Wait, you met Jack's friends tonight, didn't you?" Penny suddenly remembers.

"Yeah, I did."

"How did it go? Tell!" she says, leaning over the table. I smile back at my friend: she looks like she's going to jump across the table and onto my lap.

"Actually, it went better than I expected."

"I told you, you were way too nervous about it."

"I know."

"So, do you like them?"

"Yes, I do, especially his best friend Caleb. They became friends in Boston when they both studied there and then reconnected when they both moved to London."

"It's a small world."

"It surely is," I say, stifling a yawn.

We clear the table and go to bed, but sleep eludes me. Lallo's sad song is still playing on the back of my head when I finally close my eyes in the middle of the night.

EIGHTEEN

Friday couldn't have come fast enough. I've been so excited about my weekend away with Jack that I've been barely able to concentrate at work, daydreaming at every opportunity. Even Sarah, who's the epitome of discretion, eventually gave in and asked me what had happened to me.

I'm so happy that Jack wants to show me where he spent his childhood. My heart expands with delight at the thought that he wants to share that very private part of his life with me. I can't wait to see where he grew up… and here I go, daydreaming again.

For once, at 5.00pm sharp, I push away from my desk and wave everybody goodbye. Sarah winks at me: I told her about my little weekend break.

Back home I switch the TV on and choose a loud music channel. Penny's in Madrid for the wedding so I've had the apartment to myself for the last couple of days.

I dance around the small living room, throwing things into my little red case. As soon as I plug my phone to charge, it starts to beep. It died on me early this morning and I forgot to recharge it. Stupid battery, I mutter as I find three missed calls from my mum, one from Nico, two from unknown callers and one from Jack. Damn! I called Jack from the office this afternoon, so I'm not worried about him but I feel guilty about my mum. I'm just about to call her back when my phone rings in my hand. I frown at the display: I hate unknown callers. I turn the volume of the TV down.

"Hello?"

"Finally," says a male voice I recognize but I can't immediately place. "Lisa, it's Jude here."

"Jude," I say, surprised. When did I give Nico's band mate my number? "What's up?"

"Listen Lisa, I'm sorry to bother you but Bruce and I- well, Nico is out if it and we don't know what to do." I hear Bruce's voice, the other member of The Lost Souls, mumbling in the background. "Yeah, you see, Nico's shut down on us completely, he refuses to speak to anybody."

I'm just about to snap back that that's not my problem, but something stops me. My internal alarm sounds loudly. This can't be good. "What happened?"

"Haven't you heard?" Jude asks, surprised.

"Heard what? What are you talking about?"

I hear whispering in the background. "Jude? Are you still there?"

"Lallo died last night. He went to Italy to visit his family and was involved in a car crash."

Blood swooshes in my ears and I fall down onto the green couch, my palm pressed against my forehead.

"Lisa," says Bruce's deep voice into the phone, "please go to Nico. He doesn't answer his phone. He won't let us into his apartment. We don't know what he's doing there on his own. We're worried about him. You have to go to him."

I open my mouth to speak but no sound comes out. I think I'm in shock. Lallo, Nico, and I are childhood friends. We were. We have been friends for twenty years. Oh my God, we were.

"Lisa? Are you still there?"

"Yes, I am," I answer, shaking my head as to get out of a trance. Is this really happening?

"Will you go to Nico?"

"I- I'll call him."

"He switched his mobile off."

"I'll go now," I say breathlessly. I actually don't think there's a breath of air left in my lungs right now.

Don't panic, don't panic, don't panic, I chant in my head. I glance around my living room. Where are my keys? I snatch up my handbag and keys and run down the stairs.

The cold afternoon air hits me in the chest. I forgot to put on my jacket but I can't go back up now. I'm already running to Nico. He lives just two streets away from my place.

When we moved to London together from our little town in Italy, Nico, Lallo, and I decided to live in separate apartments, but in the same area. We wanted to give each other space, but still be neighbors, like we were in Italy. A wave of nausea rises at the bottom of my stomach but I push it away. I can't be sick here, in the middle of the street.

I approach the building where Lallo lived, which is more or less halfway between my apartment and Nico's. There are two girls standing by the entrance, holding fresh flowers, wiping their faces silently. I look down: each side of the door is covered in flowers and cards. Oh, my God, is Lallo gone for real? The girls' watery eyes meet mine and I realize I'm just standing there, staring. Somehow I resume walking towards Nico's but my legs feel heavy and a pang of pain hits me at the base of my throat. Guilt washes over me like a cold shower. Nico tried to contact me today. He probably wanted to tell me about Lallo himself, but I missed his call and never called him back, or my mother, who also obviously tried to call me to tell me about Lallo. I've been so cushioned in my soft cloud nine with Jack that I haven't been paying attention to what was happening around me. I didn't bother to look, I just didn't care. What sort of person am I?

I drag myself up the stairs of Nico's building. Lallo and I were very close, but he was also Nico's best friend, his band mate, his confidant. What if Nico lost it? He hasn't had any real loss in his life so far, I don't think he knows how to handle it.

I buzz Nico's apartment. No answer. I buzz again, more anxious by the minute. "Nico, open the door, it's me," my strangled voice says.

Still no answer. I push my ear against the cold, hard wood of the door but I can't hear anything.

"Nico!" I call louder. "Open the door!"

The door pulls away from my cheek, startling me. I gasp in shock. I barely recognize the man standing in front of me. His eyes are bloodshot and swollen; his face's pale as a sheet and his black hair disheveled. Nico looks beaten, sad; he looks lost.

He doesn't say a word. He just opens his arms and I enfold him in a long, tight, embrace that seems to last forever. Then I take a step back and walk around him into his apartment, holding back my tears. I can barely see where I'm going. It's completely dark except for the dim landing light seeping in through the front door that is still hanging open behind us. Thank God I know my way around this place. When Nico and I were together, I would spend days and days in a row here at his apartment, although he never wanted me to move in here permanently. Looking back, that feels like a very long time ago, as if it didn't happen to me but to somebody I used to know. How weird. Well, I guess nothing could make sense right now, could it?

I grab the thick fabric of the living room blinds in both my hands. "Close your eyes. I'm gonna open the blinds now." I tug the blinds open. The late afternoon golden light suddenly kisses me and I squeeze my eyes shut. I turn to find Nico sitting in my shadow on the couch, with his face buried in his hands.

For once in my life, I don't know what to do or say to him. I just stand there, helpless in front of Nico's despair, my heart squeezing in my chest. I can handle my ex when he decides to be a jerk but in all these years, I've never seen him in this state. I want to walk to him and do whatever I can to take his pain away, but this is Nico, and I know I'm threading on thin ice. I know I should keep a distance, no matter what's going on, but there's a force pulling me to him right now and it's too powerful to resist. After all, he's my childhood friend.

I sit by his side on the couch. "Nico," I say softly. He looks up at me, shaking his head, and another piece of my heart breaks. I feel my pain for Lallo rise in my chest but I push it back down, deep inside me. Not now: it would be too much to handle. You've got to be strong for Nico, I order myself. My practical side kicks in. "Nico, please, go have a shower now. Have you eaten? I'll put a light dinner together, okay? Do you have tomatoes? Cheese? Do you have anything at all to eat in this shack you live in?" I say, attempting a small smile, and failing miserably.

Nico's lips curve slightly up at my provocation, and he shakes his head again.

"All right," I say, standing on wobbling legs. "I'm gonna hop down to the shop real quick. Is there anything else you want or need?"

Something very powerful flickers in Nico's dejected eyes, but it's gone in a blink. I head for the door. "Go have a shower," I call above my shoulder, "I'll be right back."

I close the apartment door behind me, run down the stairs, and step into the crowded street. The little shop is just around the corner. What's happening? I don't really know. I'm functioning on autopilot right now. I take a basket and my eyes skim the shelves while I go through a list in my head. Tomatoes, cheese, bread, milk… My phone rings and I fish into my bag for it absently.

"Hello?"

"Baby, are you all right? Where are you?" Jack's concerned voice is a kick in the backside that brings me back to my senses. I frantically balance the basket and my phone to look at my watch: oh, God. I was supposed to meet with Jack ten minutes ago at Liverpool Street to start our lovely getaway weekend, the one I know he spent an awful amount of time planning, the one when I was supposed to meet his mother; the one I forgot about.

I forgot.

My blood turns ice-cold in my veins. How could I forget? What can I say now? I'm ashamed to admit that I quickly consider lying. But no, Jack doesn't deserve that. So I just tell the truth: that I'm shopping for Nico because he's devastated; that our childhood friend Lallo suddenly passed away and I didn't even know; that I feel terrible that I'm ruining our weekend together.

"I'm very sorry, Jack, I should have called you immediately to let you know, but everything's happening so quickly that I haven't even had a chance to get my head around it. It all just feels… tragic, surreal," I say, stifling a sob.

"I understand, baby. I'm so sorry for your loss. Where are you right now? I'll come and get you."

"No, no, it's okay."

"All right, so let me see. Our original train is leaving in three minutes, but we can probably still catch the next one… Yes, there's one leaving at half past. Can you be here in twenty minutes, baby?"

A shiver runs up my spine as I realize what Jack expects from me, where he's unintentionally pushing me. No, no, no.

"Lisa?"

"Jack, I don't think I can leave Nico like this," I hear myself say in a small voice. "He's shattered. Can't we go to Oxford another time?"

"Baby, I…How about you stay in my apartment tonight, and we leave in the morning? You can check on him again tomorrow on our way to the station, if you want."

I rub my forehead. "Jack, I- I can't leave him like this. He's my friend."

A long, uncomfortable silence falls between us. "Yeah, sure," Jack says at length. I can hear the disappointment in his controlled voice. It hurts like crazy but what can I do? I just can't leave like this.

"Jack, are you still there?"

He exhales heavily. "I'll have to catch that train. My mother's expecting us at her house tonight. It's her birthday today and she wants to have all her family around."

Oh God, today's Jack's mum's birthday. A new wave of despair hits me.

"Jack, why on earth didn't you tell me?" I all but yell into the phone as if that detail would have changed anything.

"I just wanted to surprise you but I see that wasn't a very good idea," Jack says in a clipped voice. He's slipping though my fingers, I can feel it, and yet another crack opens in my heart. "Listen, I have to go now. I'm truly sorry for your loss, although I have a feeling that this is not only about your friend passing away."

"No, Jack, please!"

"Look, Lisa, I've just offered to miss my mother's 60th birthday dinner, that my family has been organizing for months, to stay with you in London. Hell, I'd do anything for you, but you refused. You obviously don't want me around right now." I close my eyes and I imagine Jack pinching the ridge of his nose. "It's your life. You set your priorities and you've just made your choice, as simple as that. I'll just have to live with it, I guess. Just… take care of yourself, okay?

Goodbye, Lisa."

My heart shatters in one million pieces in the little shop around the corner. Is this really happening? Tears fall down my cheeks freely for the first time tonight. They are for Lallo. They are for Nico. They are for Jack and for me, and for what was between us until I crushed it a few moments ago.

"Are you all right?" an Indian shop assistant asks, and I realize I'm still clutching my dead phone to my ear. I can see why the girl's concerned: I've just lost it in her shop. I nod and manage to control my sobs with a few deep breaths. I quickly throw a few more things into my basket, pay for them, and walk the short distance to Nico's.

I let myself into Nico's apartment and find him looking out of the window. His hair is damp from a shower and he has changed into clean clothes. He doesn't even turn when I walk in: he must know it's me, that I'm here for him. I glance at my watch. The train taking Jack to Oxford is leaving the platform right now. *You should be there, sitting by his side, crying on his shoulder: he would hold you, comfort you.* No, I can't think about that right now: it's just too painful.

One by one I take the groceries out of the brown paper bag and put them on the kitchen counter.

I open the tap and let the cool water pour over the plump tomato in my hand and through my fingers. I need to shove aside my own despair at losing Lallo and my sadness for how things are going down with Jack, and try to focus on what I'm doing, on why I'm here. How can I help you, Nico? I search my head. What do I know about losing a dear one? I remember how it was when my grandma passed away. I remember the hollow that weighted on my heart for weeks: it took me a long time to shake that horrible feeling away.

I feel Nico's presence behind me; his dark shadow stretches on the wall before me and confuses with mine. Focus, Lisa, he needs to eat, I tell myself. I take the cutting board from the dish rack and place it in front of me. I slide a knife out of the knife block and slowly start to chop the red plump tomato. *Tap, tap, tap.* "Nico, what happened to Lallo…When something like that happens, you need to give yourself time.

You need to process your loss."

Nico circles my waist and puts his hands on mine. He gently opens my clenched fingers with his and I let the knife fall onto the chopping board. My heart runs at breakneck speed towards the unknown. What am I doing? Where am I going?

Nico turns me around to face him and places his palms flat on the counter on each side of me. His eyes are alive now; no, it's more than that, they are on fire. My trembling finger skims over the white little scar that splits his dark eyebrow in two, the one he got when he tried to climb the big oak tree on my grandma's hill. Lallo had almost passed out at the sight of blood trickling down his best friend's face. Did Lallo suffer when his car crashed, or was he killed instantly? Nico shivers under my touch and takes a step forward, connecting our bodies.

"Don't tell me what I need. I know exactly what I need right now," Nico drawls in Italian, shoving the cutting board to the side. With one swift movement he sits me on his kitchen counter and takes a step between my legs. He buries his face in my neck, his strong fingers digging into my hips, and my back arches automatically; bad habits die hard.

It's the despair, it's my weakness; it's our inconsiderate challenge to death. Or maybe it's just this unbearable sense of helplessness that drags me down, down, right into Nico's arms: yes, I've slipped that low and I can't find my way back up for my own life right now. Did Lallo realize that he was dying? A moan escapes my parted lips. Nico assaults my mouth, his demanding tongue plunging deep inside me, taking away what's left of my breath.

"Nico, wait," I say, but he doesn't hear me. Maybe I just whispered it too quietly; maybe the words never left my head. Nico's hands slide under my tights and I close my eyes. I don't need to see, I know exactly where he's going to take me.

NINETEEN

I wake up in full daylight to the distant sound of a guitar playing.

I push myself up on my elbows. As soon as my unfocused gaze lands on the furniture in Nico's bedroom, I feel sick to my stomach. Realization of my situation and the sorrow for Lallo's loss hit me with full force, slamming me down onto my back again. I peek down at my naked body and the magnitude of my mistake knocks the air out of my lungs. I should be in Oxford, in Jack's arms: I should be anywhere else but here, in Nico's bed.

In Nico's bed.

I scramble out of the sheets I tangled in with my ex last night, slapping one palm against my mouth to stifle a scream. Oh, my God, what have I done?

With my heart booming in my chest, I tiptoe to the half-open door on wobbly legs, and take a peek into the living room. Nico is propped on a stool, surrounded by pieces of paper scattered on the floor, a pencil hanging out of his parted lips. I see what he's doing: he survived the night and now he's pouring all his pain in his music. He'll create something very special out of this, I'm sure of that, something that will preserve Lallo's memory forever.

Nico's fingers play with the chords effortlessly. He's completely absorbed in the moment. He's far away, in a place where there's only him, his guitar, and his grief.

What is left of my self-esteem is washed away by the realization that my time with him is over. Nico's heart will grieve his friend's loss for a long time, maybe forever, but his head, the head of the artist, is already onto his next project. He doesn't need me anymore. The curtains of this exhausting on-and-off show come down again, and again, I'm on the other side: the losing one.

Bitterness builds at the base of my throat and I barely resist the urge to slam the door. My hands clench in damp fists. Why does it always have to be him dismissing me?

WHY? I scream in my head.

I slowly gather my clothes from the floor, and it has never been as humiliating as this time. Nico used me, disrupting my world just as I was trying to build something away from him, with Jack. An image of a concerned Jack waiting for me at the train station flashes up in my mind and an overwhelming wave of guilt hits me like a punch in the gut. Oh, God. How is he ever going to forgive me? I stifle a sob. Get a grip and hurry up! I scold myself. I'll need all my self-control to survive this morning's walk of shame. The last thing I want is for Nico to see my face contorting in despair: he'll surely think it's for him because, of course, it always has to be about him. I step over a torn squared foil. At least we used protection: a drop of wisdom in an ocean of idiocy. Better than nothing, I guess.

I stalk to Nico's front door without sparing him a glance. I'm so done with him and this situation.

"Wait," he says. My fingers clench around my handbag. I hold it against my stomach, as a useless, belated shield. A layer of leather surely cannot protect me from my own stupidity.

Nico puts down his guitar and walks up to me. He takes my face in his hands and kisses my temple, then the other one. "Thank you, amore," he says, touching his forehead with mine. The word *love* rolling off his tongue has never felt so wrong as in this moment, but I don't have the energy to argue with him now. I need to be gone and mourn my friend's death in peace. It's just fair that it's my turn now.

I disentangle myself from his embrace and open his front door. "Are you going to the funeral?" I ask over my shoulder.

Nico shakes his head. "They buried him this morning."

I ignore Nico's promises to call me. I just don't care if he does or not. My life is out of control and I don't even know where to begin to gather all the scattered pieces: it's just too much.

I walk towards my apartment, feeling like my shoulders weigh one ton each. This is it, back to real life. I need to mourn Lallo. I need to talk to my mother. I need to tell Jack what happened, how low I've fallen, but I don't know in which order or how. There's not much I know right now, actually.

Tears burn behind my eyes and I squeeze them hard. It's sinking in. I betrayed Jack. I crushed our relationship just while it was blossoming in my hands. I don't deserve him.

My mother's ringtone startles me. I retrieve my phone from my bag.

"Ma."

"Lisa, love, I've been calling you for two days! I was about to book a flight to London! What happened to you? Are you all right?"

Tears fall freely down my cheeks. "No, Ma, I'm not all right. I'm a mess."

"Oh, I know, baby girl, I know. He was such a lovely boy. He was family. I still can't believe it. They said he lost control of his car. It crashed against a tree. Such a lovely boy. What a waste. Teresa and Guido are shattered, poor things. Parents should never outlive their children, ever. It's against nature. It's just wrong."

"I know," I say, choking on a sob.

"Do you want me to come over to London for a few days, love? I could take a couple days off."

"Thanks Ma, but no. I'll be fine." I hate to lie to my mom but I don't want her to turn her life upside down just because her daughter is an idiot. This thought sends me into a new spiral of despair. "Did you go to the funeral?" I ask between sobs. I don't know exactly why I'm obsessing about Lallo's funeral. It's not like I regularly go to church or anything like that but I feel like everybody gathered to say their last goodbye to Lallo and I wasn't there. I should have been there.

Mom sighs heavily. "Yes, I did go to his funeral and so did the best part of town."

How ironic, I think bitterly. I'm pretty sure I don't belong to the *best* part of anything right now. I snort, disgusted with myself. I smash the pedestrian button and tap my foot on the wet pavement, cursing the red traffic light for stopping my hysterical walk.

"Where have you been for the last two days, Lisa? I was worried sick about you."

"I'm sorry, Ma, I was…"

Here we go.

"Nico and I spent some time together. It's really difficult for him, you know, to lose his best friend."

"I see," my mother says, and the way she says it makes my cheeks burn. She has guessed already. She can read me from the other side of Europe, my mum. She's the real witch, not Penny.

I rub my forehead. A rule, that's all I'm asking for: black or white, in or out. Why can't I tell what's right or wrong when it comes to Nico? Why didn't I push him away last night?

I can't believe that he's still able to draw all your attention like this. He's a damn black hole. Can't you see that he doesn't love you?

I wipe my tears away angrily.

"Whatever makes you feel better right now, Lisa, just go for it, but don't confuse a short term fix with wellbeing. You owe it to yourself to try to be happy, never forget that. You are special, baby girl; don't waste your time with people who don't deserve you."

I want to argue that I don't deserve to be happy, that I'm a shallow, stupid person; instead, I quietly accept my mother's words and store them at the back of my mind for future consideration. I don't have the strength to disagree with anything or anybody right now.

I say goodbye to my mum. It's only late morning but I've had enough of this day already. I close my apartment door behind me and let my phone ring out. I'm a coward, I know, but I can't face Jack right now. I crawl into bed in my wrinkled clothes and cry myself to sleep. I feel like I'm coming down with something. God, I just wish I were.

***

It's dark in my room when I wake up. I push myself up from the bed and my pounding head reminds me of my misery, if that was even necessary. I open my door warily. There's life on the other side. Spanish acoustic music is playing in the living room. Penny looks up from the huge book sitting on her crossed legs. She looks so normal, my Penny, so distant from pain right now. For a moment I just look down at her in silence; it's soothing. But it lasts just a few moments. She doesn't know yet, I tell myself. I can see it in her eyes that she doesn't. Is she going to freak out? How close actually were Penny and Lallo? With Miguel in the scene, I couldn't figure that out. I swallow hard in my dry mouth.

"God, Chica! You look like you've just taken a stroll through hell! What happened to you?"

"How was the wedding?" I croak out.

"Super. All my old friends from school were there. We ate like pigs and danced till morning. The vino was fantastic and abundant. Honestly, I couldn't have asked for more."

"Good," I say. I pour myself a glass of tap water. I take a sip and press my fist against my dry lips. "Penny, while you were away, something… very bad happened."

Penny takes off her hipster glasses and unfolds her legs. "What happened?"

I close my eyes. I don't want to see her face when I tell her. "Lallo… he was in a car accident. He died on Thursday night," I say in a choked voice I can barely recognize.

Penny springs off the couch, dropping her big book on the floor. She throws herself at me, stumbling over it. We just stand there, holding on to each other as if our life depended on it, sobbing like two wounded animals, with Spanish acoustic music playing softly in the background.

Penny takes a step back. "How did it happen?" Her face is red and wet. She takes a few tissues from the kitchen drawer and hands a couple to me.

"He lost control of his car. He crashed against a tree," I say, trying to pat the thin skin below my eyes dry, but fresh tears stream down, burning my sensitized cheeks.

"Hopefully he didn't suffer."

"I really hope so," I whisper.

Penny blows her nose and plops down onto our green old couch; even something so domestic, so ordinary, feels odd today. *Are you surprised, Lisa? Nothing is ever going to be the same again.*

"Lallo and I hung out a few times," Penny says at length,

fidgeting with a tissue.

"I thought so."

"Had you guessed?"

I try to smile but I only manage to twitch my lips. "Yeah, I could tell that you liked him."

"We didn't really 'see each other,' you know," she says, air-quoting. "We quite enjoyed each other's company, as friends. I think we both wished that something more could come out of it but deep down, neither of us was really into it. I think his last song is a testimony that his heart belonged to somebody else."

I blink. Does Penny know how Lallo felt about me? No, I don't think she does. He must have guessed that sharing his feelings with my closest girlfriend, the girl he was kind of seeing, wouldn't be a good idea. I mentally thank Lallo for his wisdom.

"I'm sorry if that made you sad, Penny; I mean, not really being with him."

She shakes her head. "But it didn't, because we both felt the same. I cared for Lallo as a friend, but I never really hoped for a relationship with him. Even with time, I know it wouldn't have happened."

"Because of Miguel?"

Penny casts her gaze down. "Because of Miguel."

"At least you two didn't stick together for convenience. Things were transparent between you guys and you knew where the other stood. Not that I'm surprised: you're a wonderful person and as for Lallo, well, he just wasn't like that. He wasn't a jerk."

"I know."

I take Penny's hands in mine. "Even if things had evolved between you two, he would never have used you, Penny. Trust me: I know a thing or two about being used," I say bitterly. Penny's swollen eyes dart to me and search my strained face.

"Lisa, what happened?"

I press my palms to my burning eyes.

Penny sits straighter on the couch. "Where is Jack? He's always all over you. Your phone hasn't even rang or beeped yet. He should be right here, taking care of you," she says, stabbing her finger in the green fabric.

"I- my phone is switched off."

"Why?"

"I can't talk to him right now," I say, pushing myself up. I start to pace our small living room. *Yes, Lisa, one step in front of the other, then back, just like that. And don't forget to breathe.*

"Were you in Oxford when you found out about Lallo? When did you come back?"

"I never left London. I couldn't," I say, plopping down next to her, exhausted.

I couldn't leave Nico.

I take the remote that Lallo bought for us just a few months ago. It feels like a lifetime ago. I observe the multi-colored buttons. They feel velvety under the pad of my finger.

"Did you see Nico while I was away?"

I really don't want to talk about this right now – well, make it *ever* – but I know I don't stand a chance with Penny, so I just shrug one shoulder.

"Did you… you didn't sleep with him again, did you?"

I balance the remote on my index finger. Maybe I could leave London, start afresh somewhere else, where nobody can guess what a joke of a person I am. I wonder what my grandmother would think about me if she could see how shallow I've become. She would be horrified.

Penny snatches the remote away from my hand and points it at me. Press it, Penny. Make me disappear, I don't deserve your attention, I plead silently. I think my head is about to explode.

Penny drops the remote between us. "Madre de Dios, Elisabetta, why did you do that?"

I shake my head.

"Do you still love him?"

"I will always care for Nico. He's been my world for a long, long time. I can't just erase him from my life like a dirty spot."

"But are you still *in love* him?

"No."

Penny exhales heavily. She puts her arm across my shoulders and I look back at her in surprise. "What? I will

167

always be here for you."

"Pen, I-" My throat closes. I can't even tell my friend that I don't deserve her time. I'm such a loser. Instead, I bury my face in her slim shoulder and cry my eyes out all over again.

TWENTY

Today is the first day of summer; it is also the fourth day without Lallo walking in this world.

When I was a little girl, this time was the happiest of the year. Yes, for us kids, it was better than Christmas day. School ended at the beginning of summer and Lallo, Nico, and I would start to pack our favorite t-shirts and toys to go spend the warmest season at my grandma's farm.

It feels like a lifetime ago.

I had the strangest dream last night. I dreamt that Lallo was knocking at a huge brass door, in the middle of nowhere. The door opened and my grandma stood there, young as I remember her when we were kids. She opened her arms and smiled at him. She was always a sweet woman, my nana. Seeing how she was accepting Lallo made me hope that he's not on his own, wherever he is.

I blink and resume putting on some makeup but there's not much I can do to cover up my puffy eyes. I give up and throw the mascara tube back into my makeup bag. I'm so tempted to call in sick today; after all, God knows I've never felt worse in my life. But my sense of duty makes me drag myself out of the apartment.

The morning light stings my eyes. I forgot my sunglasses. I quickly step down into the artificially-illuminated underground station, wishing that the big crowd of commuters would swallow me up, but I have no such luck, unfortunately.

I get off the train in the city center, but not at my usual stop. Jack and I are meeting up for breakfast, 'to talk.' I don't even know why he is still speaking to me. Oh, yeah. He doesn't know yet that I slept with Nico the other night. I shiver runs up my spine. This is so, so bad. I absolutely dread the moment I have to tell him, and the consequences of my reckless actions.

I locate him immediately, the most handsome man in the already busy café. I would spot him in the blink of an eye among one million people. He is always his impeccable self. If only I could say that about myself. *Then you wouldn't need to humiliate yourself and hurt this man this morning, Lisa, would you?*

I pull out the chair in front of Jack warily and sit down. He searches my face, in silence. The speech I played in my head all night long suddenly fades away, and I'm completely lost. How do you confess a terrible mistake? Do you get straight to the point, or go round and round what you want to say, until the other person gets it on his own? How do you discharge a bomb right on the man you love and save anything good that was between the two of you?

The man you love.

"I'm so sorry for your loss, baby," Jack says, pulling me back to the café. "I shouldn't have left you on your own in London. I thought about you the entire time that I was away anyway."

"Oh, Jack."

"What would you like?" he asks, gently, handing me the menu. I would like to rewind the last few days of my life. I would like Lallo to still be alive. I would like to be wiser. Can you arrange for that to happen, Jack?

"I'm okay, thanks," I say, pressing a hand to my churning stomach.

"How do you feel now?" he asks, his hand reaching out to me and threading through my hair. I lean into his touch. I know it's selfish, I know I don't deserve Jack's comfort, but I can't help myself. Just this last time.

"Jack, I'm so sorry."

"Don't apologize, baby. This was a terrible tragedy. I understand."

"No, you don't. I wasn't on my own here."

"You weren't?" he asks, pulling his hand back to his side of the table. I shake my head, already feeling the loss of his touch.

He blinks. "I don't understand. What are you saying?"

My heart is galloping in my throat, ready to jump out any minute. "I spent Friday night at Nico's," I blurt out.

Jack stares at me in shock. "You did what?"

My cheeks burn and I feel my heart is going to explode any moment now. I cast my glance down in shame and wait for the

170

blow that I know is coming.

"Did you sleep with him?"

Oh, my God.

"Jack, I'm so sorry, I never meant for things to go that way."

"Lisa, I'm gonna ask you again: did you or did you not sleep with him?"

I nod.

"Say it."

"Yes," I whisper.

Jack puts his coffee down and slowly leans over the table.

"Let me get this right. Are you saying that while I was holding back to give you space, to make it special for us, you've been fucking your ex-boyfriend behind my back all along?"

I jerk on my chair. I don't know this guy who's swearing at me. I only know the sweet, understanding Jack. I've never seen him like this: he's furious and outraged, and very rightly so. A new pang of guilt hits me. I put those vulgar words on his lips. It's my fault.

"Jack, please, I beg you to believe me. It happened only once. Since you came into my life, I have only been trying to avoid him."

Jack's eyes flare. "Did he… force himself on you?"

Oh, dear God.

I shake my head no, my cheeks turning a darker shade of pink, if that's even possible. I can no longer speak: I'm on the verge of bursting into tears.

"What a fucking bastard," Jack mutters under his breath, "and you…" He stops midsentence then his expression transforms into a sober, flat one. He pins me with his clear blue eyes. They are as cold as ice slots. The force of his gaze pierces through me and my breath catches in my lungs. "At least you admitted it. The last one didn't even have the decency to give me that closure when I found her half naked next to her bed. With her *friend* sprawled out on it."

Oh, no!

"Jack, I made a terrible error of judgment, I'm so very

sorry."

"No, Lisa, *I* made a terrible error of judgment. I thought we had something special. I have a hard time trusting women, but I thought you were different. I even told you that I can't tolerate dishonesty, for Christ's sake. But you just proved to me that being prudent is never enough."

My eyes finally fill with tears at the realization that, on top of everything, I shattered Jack's attempt to trust again. He doesn't deserve that, or anything else that I've thrown at him.

"Jack, I'm so sorry, I wish I could turn back time."

"At least I dodged becoming your rebound. Just barely," he says, throwing a few bills on the table. His phone rings and he takes it out of his pocket. "Jackson Kendall," he says, in his best professional tone. "Yes, thank you. I'll be right out." He puts his phone back into his pocket, stands up, and retrieves a small suitcase from behind his chair.

"Are you going away?" I croak out. Wherever you're going, you're taking my heart with you, Jackson Kendall. Do you even know?

"I'm going to Paris on a business trip. If you hadn't been so busy in bed with your ex when I called, I would have told you that, and to pack a bag and go with me; I wanted to take you away from your pain, even if for just a few days." He pushes his hand through his short hair. "I was falling in love with you, Lisa. Now I can see how stupid I've been."

Jack turns on his heel and walks away from me. I clench my napkin in my hand. How could my world spin on its axes so quickly? *You pulled that lever yourself, Lisa. Now you can't expect to just bring it back to place over coffee.*

I sit at the table of the café for a few more moments, to make sure Jack is gone. I'm probably the last person he wants around right now. I retrieve my phone from my bag with trembling hands. There's one more missed call that I need to return: another impossible conversation, another exceptional person in my life to let down.

"Lisa, honey, how are you? I've been sick worried about you since Jack walked through Aunt Liz's door without you on Friday!" Nancy's concerned voice drifts out of my phone and a

new wave of despair hits me hard.
   One more person to let down.

TWENTY-ONE

"So, what do you think?"

I glance at Sarah's fidgeting hands and back at my laptop's screen.

"I love it."

"Do you?"

"I absolutely do. You have excellent taste. These decorations will make a huge difference, for the better."

She shrugs. "Nobody will care anyway; it's just a bunch of tablecloths and napkins."

"No, Sarah. It's pale yellow tablecloths and cream napkins, coordinated plates and glasses and a combination of peach-orange roses and sunflowers. It's about decorating the party venue using a clever color palette that will create a summer vibe in the room, whatever the weather outside. And it's about your great attention to detail and the effort you put into this."

"It was your idea to have a color pattern for the venue."

"Yes, but the colors you chose are perfect. In event management, execution is as important as the idea itself, if not more."

"But-"

I hold up my hand. "Honey, really, enough with this self-deprecation. Why can't you just accept a compliment and recognize that you've done a good job?" I ask gently.

Sarah shrugs. "I know you're right, I'm sorry. I'm being as sulky as a three-year-old. I barely slept last night. Mike worked the night shift and Molly decided to wake up every two hours. I guess I'm a bit out of kilter today. Sleep deprivation is a form of torture, after all."

"It's all right, let's just go ahead and confirm everything with the catering company, okay? The efficient one you selected, by the way."

I mirror Sarah's tired smile and close my laptop. I didn't sleep a wink last night, either. How could I, with all that's been going on? Thank God for my job: it makes me drag myself out of bed every morning and gives me perspective at this difficult time when everything else seems to be crumbling and falling around me.

I push away from my desk, slide into my jacket, and wave everybody goodbye. How I wish I could indulge in the comfort zone of my office all day today.

It was my dread of this afternoon that kept me up all night last night. I shiver at the idea of facing the tangible reality of Lallo's passing; it's just too much pain. But I couldn't say no. I mean, how can you say no to a dad who asks for a favor between choked sobs? I've known Guido all my life, but when he called me the other night, I could barely make out his words, so strained was his voice. So we cried together and here I am now, heading to Lallo's apartment to go through his stuff. I wondered why Lallo's parents didn't ask Nico to handle this. Mum says that they must have thought that a woman would do a better job, be more careful with their son's things.

I wipe my eyes. I've never been the weepy kind but drying my tears with the back of my hands has become a frequent gesture for me lately, with Lallo gone and Jack avoiding me. I refuse to carry tissues in my purse, though; I know it's silly, but I feel it would be like giving in to the pain, accepting that I lost both my friend and my love in the span of forty-eight hours. Honestly, I'm not there yet.

Denise is coming to Lallo's with me. She insisted I not go alone: she says I would dissolve into tears; she's probably right. I lean against the cold marble wall and tilt my head back into the sun. It's a fresh, clear summer day, one of those without clouds in the sky.

The swirling door moves and I glance down at two men walking out of Denise's office building. They are in deep conversation. One is grey-haired and is holding a tablet, and the other one… Oh, no. It's Martin-the-Nordic-god. I so don't need this now. Martin shoves his hands in his black suit trouser pockets; when he notices me, he looks me up and down and arches a brow. With nowhere to hide, I cringe in my little leather jacket. Thank God the men don't slow their pace and keep walking towards Starbucks on the other side of the road.

"There you are," says Denise, her stilettos tapping rhythmically as she walks up to me, her eyes trailed on the men's backs until they disappear into the coffee shop. Then she tucks a strand of hair behind my ear, searching my eyes. "He didn't try to talk to you, did he?"

"Who? Martin?"

"Yes."

I shake my head. "Thank God, he was too busy speaking with somebody else."

"Hmm mmm."

"He hasn't got past the pub incident, has he?"

Denise's lips purse in a thin line.

"I'm so sorry."

My friend waves a hand dismissively. "He just has a big ego. Golden boys tend to."

"Jack isn't like that," I say, without thinking. Denise puts an arm across my slouched shoulders and we walk in silence to the parking lot.

Twenty minutes later, Denise pulls over just in front of what used to be Lallo's home. All the flowers and the cards that his fans left to say goodbye are gone. I wonder who has them. Maybe Teresa and Guido would want to keep the cards.

"Do you have the cards that people left for Raffaello?" I ask the landlord.

"No, I don't; I gave them to a friend of his."

"To whom?" Denise asks.

"Nicolas Neri, I think his name is. Raffaello put him down as his emergency contact when he signed the contract for the apartment, so I figured I should give the cards to him."

We ride up to the second floor and the landlord unlocks the door. It's dark in the apartment. Of course, Lallo would have closed all windows and curtains, because he was going away for a few days; he was meant to go only for a few days. Just for a few days... A light flicks on, then another one in the bedroom.

"I'll be back in about four hours. I don't mean to put you under pressure, especially under these tragic circumstances, but I need the place cleared by tonight. The agency has arranged a viewing tomorrow and I can't afford to keep the apartment empty for long, you know," the landlord says, apologetically.

"We understand," Denise says. "Are there any boxes we can use?"

The landlord points to a pile of flattened boxes against the wall to our right. "Just use as many as you need and leave everything by the door. I'll get the boxes labeled and collected first thing in the morning." He stops at the threshold and looks over his shoulder. "Thank you for taking care of this. I'm sorry for your loss. Your friend was a model tenant."

He's gone before I can say anything; my reaction time hasn't been the quickest lately.

I look around the small living room. I haven't been here in a long time. Lallo's small desk is covered in music books and notepads; next to it, his complete drum set and a big bongo are sitting neatly. An electronic keyboard fills the space under the window: that must be a recent acquisition. I guess that working at the music store had its perks, after all. He covered the keys with a cloth to preserve it from dust. I smile to myself. This room is so much him. It's the room of a tidy musician; it *was*, rather. Everything will have to go. Tenuous whiffs of Lallo's cologne, that's all that will be left of him in his place by tomorrow.

On the wall next to the window hangs a frame: it's a collection of pictures I had never noticed before. There's one of Lallo playing the drums on stage, his head tilted back, his eyes closed, as if was praying to a god above. There's one of him with the band, their instrument boxes scattered around them. In another one, Lallo's sitting and Nico is standing behind him, holding him in a headlock: they are smiling. And then there's a small, scratched picture of the three of us: Lallo, Nico and I, sitting cross-legged on the grass in our colorful summer shorts. The boys are bare-chested; I'm wearing a pink tank top and my hair is combed in pigtails. We are grinning at the camera, showing off our popsicles: to my grandma, I'm sure. I trace my finger on the cold glass and my vision blurs.

I feel Denise's comforting hand on my shoulder. Her touch is gentle, soothing. "Where do we start?"

I wipe my eyes and glance towards the bedroom. With a box in her hand, she walks into the bedroom and sets to work. I take a steadying breath and join her.

Denise and I work in silence, removing Lallo's t-shirts and jumpers from drawers and shelves and carefully piling them into boxes. Have you ever gone through somebody's things without their permission? It's invasive. I feel like I'm trespassing.

"Life is crazy," Denise murmurs, absently. She's thinking aloud.

We hear a noise in the living room.

"I'll go check, Denise says, standing up. "Maybe the landlord forgot something." I hear muffled voices; then Denise walks back into the bedroom.

"Nico is here," she says, grimly. My pulse jumps as he appears behind her.

"Lisa."

"What are you doing here?"

He shoves his hands deep into his pockets. "Guido told me you would be going through Lallo's stuff this afternoon. I thought I would help."

"I'll be in the living room if you need me," Denise says, glaring at Nico.

Nico's eyes dart around the room, warily. "So, what do you want me to do?"

I look up at him for a long moment. "I want you to understand that there's a reason why I asked you not to call me for a while. You shouldn't be here. I need space."

"Lisa, I-"

"I need space."

"I know, but-"

"But what, Nico? Why are you here?" I ask, louder than I intended. He gazes out of the window above my head and cracks his neck. "I asked you why you are here," I hiss.

"I wanted to see you."

I rub my forehead. "Why, Nico? Where is this urgency to see me coming from?"

"I've been thinking- I just wanted to see how you were

doing."

"Why?"

"Well, after you came to my place and we-"

"After you used me, once again? Is your conscience bothering you, all of a sudden?" I yell.

"I didn't *use* you: you were consenting and you were there with me, all the way."

I push up from the bed on trembling legs, my heart in my throat. "Nicolas, you've been using me physically and emotionally since you dumped me. You texted, called, and showed up for months, interfering in my life, putting a strain on my new relationship, and now-"

"Hold on there, Elisabetta, I-"

"I will not hold on here! You're such a selfish bastard! Are you denying that you've been using me?"

"I've been texting, calling, and showing up; and you've been texting me back, taking my calls, and sleeping with me. You're a big girl, Lisa: you've been with me of your own will. Just don't blame me now if you regret your choices."

"How dare you!"

Nico pushes away from the wall and points his finger down at me. "I never forced you to do anything, anything at all: it was your decision. It's true, I pursued you because I needed you, but you needed me, too. When you were on your own, whenever you were down, it's me you came to, for Christ's sake! *Me!*" Nico says, stabbing his wide chest with his finger. "Now, tell me, Lisa: who's been using who?"

I gape at my ex. He's never spoken to me like this before. He threads his hands through his hair. "Look, Lisa, I'm sorry. I really am, for everything. Just… stop playing the blame game, please. You know better. There's no black or white here: reality is much more complicated than that." He cups my face, his thumbs skimming over my tear-streaked cheeks. "I'm sorry, amore. Don't cry. I can't stand it when you cry." His arm falls to his side then he turns and leaves without another word.

My legs give in and I collapse onto Lallo's bed. Stop crying, Lisa, I tell myself, but I can't: my confrontation with Nico has wreaked havoc in my mind and in my heart, leaving me in a precarious emotional state.

I suddenly feel an overwhelming need to call Jack. I need to hear his voice, to feel the warm comfort of his kindness. I need him to tell me that everything will be all right.

I bury my head in my hands. Jack hasn't been returning my calls for days, but he was in Paris last week and I haven't tried to reach him for twenty-four hours now… maybe if I call him at the office instead of on his mobile, he'll take my call. I reach for my purse and fish blindly for my phone.

"Remington, Gibson & Partners, good afternoon, how can I help you?"

"I'm looking for Jackson Kendall, please." Oh God, please, let him be in the office, please, please, please…

"Mr. Kendall is not in London, I'm afraid. May I ask who's speaking?"

I rub my forehead. "It's Lisa Castelli, his… his friend. When will he be back from Paris?"

"He came back from Paris four days ago, madam, and then he moved office. He flew out this morning."

My blood freezes in my veins. "He moved? Where did he move to?"

"He moved back to New York. Would you like me to give you the number of our office in Manhattan? Hello, madam?"

My phone slips from my hand and bounces onto Lallo's bedspread noiselessly.

TWENTY-TWO

Life without Lallo is tough; life without Lallo and Jack is complete, utter hell.

Seven weeks have passed since *s-night*. The night I slept with Nico even though I was with Jack, the night I touched rock bottom: *s* for shame, for shattering, for how stupid I acted; *s* for this sadness that I carry on my shoulders and I can't shake off; *s* for selfish. That's what Nico fundamentally is, and I'm no better than him.

I shift uncomfortably on the hard wood and look up; the sky is heavy with summer rain. It's just a matter of time and it will pour down on me, on the bench I'm sitting on in Exchange Square in the heart of London City. This is where Jack worked when he lived here. It would be an impersonal world of glass and steel frames if it weren't for Jack. Instead, this is where he spent the best hours of his days and fulfilled himself as a young manager. Jack had this power to make everything and everybody around him better, except me, I guess.

I haven't been well, these past weeks. I've been trying to come to terms with what has happened but when things go down so suddenly and quickly, it's difficult to comprehend and adjust.

Penny walks up to me with two ice-cream cups she insisted on buying to cheer me up. Of all places, I dragged her here today, where I would sometimes meet with Jack for lunch, when the time we spent together was never enough.

"This place makes you sad," Penny says, sitting down next to me.

"That's right. That's why I'm here."

"But why? That's something about you I don't get. Why do you keep on tormenting yourself like this?"

"Because I deserve it, Penny; because I'm the master of my own unhappiness."

She rolls her eyes. "So that's it? You're gonna slowly roast in your private little hell for the rest of your days?"

"It's not all bad, you know."

"It isn't? Do you mean there's something positive coming out of all this mess? Illuminate me, please, because all I see around you is the pitch dark sorrow you're swimming through."

"I made many mistakes and I'm learning from them. That doesn't happen overnight. I now understand that blaming Nico for what happened is not the answer. I may not have initiated our last encounter, but it takes two to tango. And I wouldn't have been there that night, in Nico's apartment, if only I had realized earlier how much I really cared about Jack. So you see, it's a learning process. I just wish I hadn't had to sacrifice what Jack and I had to get to the place I am today."

"I'm relieved that it's finally over between you and Nico," Penny says, digging into her ice-cream.

"Nico and I are not meant to be, after all. I care about him, I always will, but I don't love him. It's Jack I love."

Penny exhales heavily. "So why don't you call him and tell him how you feel? You should've done that weeks ago. You're so stubborn."

"Pen, you know how I feel about calling him. He's far away, living his life without me. Maybe he has somebody else now," I say, swallowing hard. "It would be very selfish of me to bother him, don't you think?"

"But Nancy said he's single, didn't she?"

Yes, she did; she told me one night when I was crying on her shoulder because I missed her cousin. I think she took pity on me.

Nancy's understanding in all this big, nasty mess touched me deeply. She knew about Jack's previous relationship, that it had ended because of Jack's ex-girlfriend cheating on him. When I confessed what I had done, she asked me how I could do something like that to Jack. I told her the truth: that to this day, I'm not completely sure what happened that night between me and Nico. What I know for sure is that it had nothing to do with my ex and I rekindling, and everything to do with us handling the shock of Lallo's sudden death. Still, what I did was wrong and I can't believe she was able to forgive me, after all; generosity obviously runs in her family.

"I think you should give yourself a chance, Chica. You think you know what Jack will say when you open your heart to him, that he will reject you, but in reality you don't know that; nobody does, until it happens. You think Jack will despise you forever because you're so harsh on yourself, but I think you're underestimating him. He's a smart, sensitive man."

I half-smile at Penny with gratitude. How many times has she tried to restore my faith in the world over the last two months? I lost count. She's been my rock, despite her own efforts to mourn Lallo. I glance down at the pink melted ice-cream in my cup; it's watered down with rain now. I wish Jack would accept my apologies and forgive me, but I guess that too much has happened to start afresh.

"Lisa, come on, you'll catch a cold in this rain!" Penny says, motioning for me to follow her. We run for the shelter of a café. Memories flash in my mind of the night when Jack asked me to go to Oxford. It was pouring, just like now. But what does it matter if it's melting hot or snowing, when you're happy? A new pang of pain hits me at that thought, but I'm stronger now. I have to be, because everything reminds me of Jack. I miss him like crazy.

"Vamos, Chica," Penny says as soon as the rain subsides. "Visiting time starts in thirty minutes and we don't wanna miss a second of it, do we now?"

***

"Aww, look at him, he's perfect!" Penny says. Baby Patrick blinks, stirs in Monique's arms, and then snuggles against his mummy's breasts again.

"He's beautiful, guys, congratulations again," I say.

"He has my eyes," Andy says, puffing his chest.

Nancy throws her head back and laughs.

"Ah, shut up, Andy! Your son is twelve hours old. He's blinked twice since he was born, and his eye color is not there yet, anyway," Monique says.

Andy mutters something then he arranges the pillows

behind his fiancé's back and kisses the top of her head.

"We brought you Swiss chocolate," I say, showing Monique a big chocolate box. My friend's eyes roll back in delight.

"Have I ever told you that I love you? Put them there, honey, please. I'll have one as soon as I put the little monkey in his cot."

"I'll take care of that box," Andy says, a little too enthusiastically.

"Don't you dare to touch my chocolate, Andy O'Brien! Those treats are mine. God knows I deserved them. I did all the hard work last night while you were passed out!" Yes, Andy passed out in the delivery room, poor thing. But when he came to his senses, he refused to leave Monique's side until his son was born safely into the world.

"Fair play to you for staying by your family's side," I tell him sincerely. He winks, making us all laugh. Ah, Andy!

"Monique, I'll just move these lovely flowers to the side to make space for the box, is that okay?" I ask.

"Sure, go ahead, honey."

"These are truly gorgeous. Who sent them?" Denise asks, gently skimming her fingers over the delicate petals.

Monique looks up at me apologetically. "Jack brought them earlier."

My heart skips a beat. From across the room, Nancy smiles at me.

"He did?" Penny asks in surprise, her eyes darting to mine.

"Yes. He's actually gone to the shop downstairs to buy me cookies. I've been craving them since yesterday afternoon, but Andy won't leave his son's side," Monique says, her cheeks turning pink. If my heart wasn't about to jump out of my ribcage, I would make a comment about how adorable she looks right now, holding her newborn in her arms, blushing over a pack of cookies; but all I can think about is that the man I love is somewhere in this building. So close.

"Monique, do you feel like having a few shots taken?" Miguel asks over Penny's shoulder. Monique threads her hand through her curls self-consciously. "Natural shots are the best," he says gently.

"All right then, thanks," she answers coyly.

We all move to the back of the room and watch in fascination how Miguel angles his camera and click after click captures the magic of this young new family.

I glance at Penny sideways: she's in love with Miguel, there's no doubt about that. I guess that one of the few positive things about the tragedy of Lallo's death is that it made us all reflect on how short life is. This is something we young people underestimate. It was a true wake-up call for Penny and made her reconsider her relationship with Miguel. Since she let her guard down, she's been glowing with happiness.

A soft knock comes from behind the door and I stiffen. I look over my shoulder and there is Jack, filling the door with his big frame, just like the first time we met. I shove the memories away and try to smile. To my utter surprise, his lips curve up. It's a small but kind smile, one of those that knock the air out of your lungs because you don't expect them, or deserve them. I turn back to watch Miguel working but all I can think about is Jack, and how much I love him. How have I survived all this time without him?

"Let's take a walk in the park," he whispers in my ear.

We walk down the long impersonal corridor of the hospital, but we could be anywhere. I don't see where I'm going. All I hear is the thud of my heart in my ears; I can barely breathe.

We step out into the warm summer sun and find a free bench under a huge chestnut tree. I slide on the bench next to Jack, keeping what I guess is a respectable distance, fighting the instinct to sit on his lap. God, he's even more beautiful than I remember.

"How have you been?" he asks at length. When I just shake my head, he looks surprised. "You lost weight," he says, disapproval showing clearly in his voice and frown. "Doesn't he make you happy?"

I look up at him in confusion. "Who?"

"Nico."

"Nico and I haven't met since we cleared Lallo's apartment just after he died."

"You two aren't together?" he asks in disbelief.

I shake my head. "That's not what that night at Nico's was about. It wasn't about getting back together."

Jack looks me straight in the eye. His expression is flat but I can see the muscle in his jaw jumping.

"Look, Jack, I know I let you down. You probably have a hard time believing anything I say to you now, and I don't blame you, but Nico and I never meant to get back together. That's not why we did what we did that night."

"I don't know what you are saying."

"Jack, please, try to understand: I was in despair, disoriented, things got out of control. I'm not in love with Nico, I haven't been for a long time. I could never get back with him. He's not the one I want."

Tell him, Lisa, tell him how you feel about him, the little voice in my head prompts me. Why is it so difficult?

Because his rejection would destroy you.

Jack stares at me and I can see all the conflicting emotions playing on his handsome face. He's trying to protect himself, but he wants to believe what I said. I cover his hand with mine on impulse. The sensation of our skins touching is so intense that I need to close my eyes, just for a moment, to savor it and get a grip at myself. I open my eyes and they lock with his now softer ones. "Will you be in London for long?"

"I moved back here last week."

"You did?" I ask in surprise. "But Nancy said… I just thought that your move to New York was permanent."

"It was meant to be, but I…" He skims his fingers over my check and oh, my heart does a double flip. "Do you… have plans for tonight?"

I shake my head.

"Come have dinner to my place."

"Where do you live now?"

"In my old apartment; I couldn't bring myself to sell it."

A chance, that's all I'm asking for, and hopefully Jack is giving it to me. The lyrics of the song that Lallo wrote for me play back in my head, just as if he was sitting on the bench here with us right now, singing them softly.

Now I know I can't be your man, ever,
But promise me,
That you'll fight for the one you love,
It's today or never.

***

I'm a bundle of nerves as I ride on the elevator of Jack's building. I still can't believe that he's back in London, or that I'm going to have dinner at his place tonight.

I skim my damp palms over my skirt. It took me three hours to get ready for this date: too elegant, too casual nothing looked appropriate. Well, I'm not even sure if this is a date or not actually, but I'm not going to overthink it. All I want right now is to see Jack again, to touch his skin, just to make sure he's back for real.

The elevator chimes and I step out on wobbling legs. Maybe going for high-heeled sandals wasn't the best idea after all. But when you have only one last bullet to shoot, you try to aim for your best, right? I just hope that I won't embarrass myself by falling flat on my face.

Before I can knock on Jack's door, he opens it. Oh my God. He's a vision in a red t-shirt and faded jeans that sit low on his hips. His gaze trails down my body and back up. I hold my breath: I hope he likes what he sees. He takes my hand and gently tugs me into his apartment, closing the door behind us.

"Hi, gorgeous," he says, locking his arms around my waist. I wrap mine around his neck, holding on for dear life. If I'm dreaming right now, I never want to wake up.

Jack's delicious, familiar scent blends with the one of homemade food and a vision flashes in my head of how it would feel to come home to his arms every night, to hold each other like this, in our home. A sense of belonging sets in my chest. It just feels right to be here, with Jack, savoring every second of his warm embrace. "Thank you for inviting me here. I missed you so much," I say against his shoulder.

"So did I, baby. No matter the distance I tried to put between us, I couldn't get you out of my head."

Is Jack giving me another chance? Can he really do that? Am I strong enough to take up this challenge?

I clench my fingers in Jack's hair and pull his parted lips down to mine, but he stiffens one inch away from my mouth.

"Is he finally out of your system?" he drawls.

I blink in surprise.

"Is he?" he asks fiercely, shaking me out of my silence.

"Yes, yes he is."

His gaze falls to my lips. "This is a one-way ticket, Lisa. This is your last chance to back out. Are you sure?"

"Yes, I am," I say. "There's you, only you now."

Jack growls then his head falls down to mine and I pour all my heart in a white hot kiss that goes on and on and on. He takes his time to devour my mouth, his tongue tangling with mine in the most sensual and ancient of dances. His big hands skim down my back to cup my buttocks and my head falls back in pleasure.

"In the bedroom, now," Jack orders. He scoops me up swiftly, making me shriek in surprise and delight. Oh, I quite like caveman Jack.

He lowers me onto his bed gently and undresses me between wet, delicious kisses that make me shiver from head to toe.

From his bed, I watch in awe as Jack takes his t-shirt and jeans off. By the time he has disposed of his clothes, I'm panting. "Perfection," I murmur under my breath. When his boxers go at last, my breath catches and I lick my lips. Jack stands there, hard and proud, looking down at me with burning eyes, and time stops. That's it, I tell myself. After tonight, you'll never be the same woman again.

Jack kneels on the silky navy bedspread, bracing one strong arm on each side of me. I skim my palms up his forearms, over his shoulders, and down his chest, enjoying the warmth of his smooth skin.

"You're so beautiful, baby. A goddess."

I smile coyly, watching under my lashes how his hand takes

its time to caress every hill and valley of my body, spurring my racing heart into a wild gallop.

"This will have to be hard and fast, baby. I've been waiting for too long," he says roughly, shifting over me. He searches in the nightstand drawer and readies himself. "Are you ready for me, love? Can you handle me?" he asks, skimming his fingertips over my quivering belly.

Oh, yes, YES! "Yes, I'm ready for you, Jack," I say, breathlessly.

Jack lowers himself between my legs. He kisses my temple, my jaw, and with his face buried in the side of my neck, he enters me with one deep thrust that makes me cry out in bliss.

"You feel so good, baby. So warm and tight," he growls, moving over me to allow me to adjust to his invasion.

"Oh, Jack. Jack." I dig my fingernails in his flesh, asking for more.

"Say it again," he commands. "Say my name."

Lost in the moment and in the feel of our joined bodies, I chant his name like a prayer. He plunges into me once, twice, over and over again, stretching my body and my heart to the limit. He's claiming his woman, he's marking my body permanently. It's hard and primal and there's nothing I want or need more. My back arches and I meet each one of his powerful thrusts as if my next breath depended on it; it probably does.

Liquid burning pleasure pools deep in my belly and my breath catches. Just when I think that I can't last much longer, Jack suddenly stalls inside of me and a moan leaves my parted lips. I open my eyes, just in time to see the amazing rainbow of emotions playing on his face. All I need to know is right there, shining in his smoldering blue eyes. Passion. Tenderness. Love.

Jack moves again, but slowly now and I realize in awe that each one of his long thrusts is stroking my soul. He did it: he reached the deepest fold of my being. A tear falls from the corner of my eye as he locks his fingers with mine.

"You okay?" he asks, tenderly.

I nod.

"Come for me, baby," he whispers, and takes my mouth in

another hungry kiss.

The most consuming pleasure I've ever felt in my life hits me like lightning and I cry out against his mouth. Jack pushes into me one last, powerful time, launching us both into ecstasy.

We lie in bed, satiated and spent. Jack's weight on my limp body feels wonderful. I can't say where I end and where he starts: I never want to know. My fingertips trail lazy patterns on the velvety skin of his back while our pulses slow down.

"I'm sorry, I'm crushing you."

"No, baby, I love to feel you so close to me."

Jack smiles sheepishly and rolls to his side, holding me tight. I snuggle as close to him as humanly possible, cocooned in my man's warmth and exquisite scent.

My man.

He threads his hand through my tousled tresses. "I love you, Lisa. I don't mind if you can't say it back right now, as long as you feel it in your heart."

"Oh, Jack."

"Don't cry, baby," he says, wiping my tears with his thumb but I can't contain myself. You can't hold back tears of joy.

"Ti amo, Jackson Kendall. I love you so much."

He brings our entwined hands to his mouth and kisses each of my knuckles, making me shiver with pleasure. What I feel with Jack surpasses anything I've ever known, by far. I whisper under my breath in Italian, lost in the sensation. With one swift movement, Jack flips me to my back. "Do it again," he says, roughly, mischief dancing in his eyes.

"What?"

"Say may name and that other thing in Italian. It's sexy as hell."

"Stai con me per sempre, Jack."

"What does it mean?" he asks against my slightly-parted lips.

"It means *stay with me forever.*"

Jack looks into my eyes with an intensity that makes my toes curl. "Elisabetta Castelli, you will be the end of me." He lowers his mouth onto mine and we lose ourselves in each other all over again, our dinner forgotten. Again.

TWENTY-THREE

"Great job, Ladies! Bravissime!" Mr. Conrad says enthusiastically, raising his glass of white wine. Sarah and I clink our glasses with our boss's and grin at each other.

The summer party has been a success and, thank God, it's finally wrapping up. It's late afternoon, after all. "I'm beat," Sarah says as soon as Mr. Conrad is out of sight, plopping down on a chair. "Let's shove all these people out of here and head home. I couldn't walk another minute in these traps," she says, taking off her high heels and sighing in delight.

I chuckle and take a sip from my glass. I can't wait to go back into my boyfriend's arms, where I belong. That has been my favorite part of the day, every day, since we got back together one month ago.

"Lisa?"

"Mmh?"

"Thank you," Sarah says.

"For what, honey?" I ask in surprise.

"For helping me settle back in my work routine. It's not easy to go back to work after you've just had a baby, you know. It's tiring. It takes time to ramp up again after being off for almost a year and all sorts of insecurities gnaw at you. I guess it's out of guilt for leaving your child in somebody else's care for so many hours every day," she says, pensively. "I understand now why Mr. Conrad gave me the opportunity to work with you. You are great. I was a mess when we started working on this project and look at me now: I'm the queen of the GBG summer party," she says, striking a pose in her chair.

I throw my head back and laugh. "You don't need to thank me, Sarah. You did it all on your own," I say, winking.

My phone beeps in my pocket. A text from Nico flashes on the screen.

Hey, I need to talk to you. Please come over to my place. I'm in trouble

I stiffen, unwanted memories of my last encounter with Nico flashing in my head. Nico hasn't been fishing for my attention for weeks now, but still…what I have with Jack is real and it's perfect. I don't want to jeopardize it in any way, I quickly type my answer back.

I really can't. I'm sorry

Nico's answer flashes on my screen immediately.

I wish that Lallo was here. He's the one I'd have turned to. I can't believe I put myself in this situation

Oh. This makes me pause. As sneaky as Nico can be, he wouldn't mention Lallo to get my attention, would he? Nico must be really in trouble: my protective side kicks into overdrive.

Now, you may think I'm a silly softie, and with all what's happened, well, I see where you're coming from. But this is the thing: Nico is no longer my boyfriend or my lover, but he'll always be my childhood friend; the only one left. Maybe I could spare a few minutes to hear what he's panicking over tonight. Only this time I'm going to discuss this with Jack beforehand and thoroughly.

***

"Why can't you meet him in a public place? Why does he want you to go to his place?" Jack asks me for the third time in half an hour.

"He said he feels uncomfortable speaking about this is public."

"But why?"

"I don't know, baby."

"I'll go with you."

I hold my hand up. "We've already discussed this, Jack. I will not be escorted around London because you don't trust me."

Jack purses his lips and nods. "Fair point; but don't think that I don't trust you. It's *him* that I don't trust at all."

I take a step forward and lock my arms around Jack's neck.

"Don't do that."

"What?" I ask.

"Try to bribe me into agreeing that you meet him at his

place; that's not gonna happen."

"Baby, please. I know I'm asking a lot, but you have to trust me. How can we be together in the long run if you don't trust me?"

Jack frowns down at me. I hate that I've put that troubled look in his eyes and I'm worried that he will go back into distrust zone: if he decides to indulge himself there, our relationship will be crushed. But at the same time, in my heart of hearts, I know that Jack and I cannot really build a future together if he thinks that I'm going to fall into Nico's arms ever again.

I count mentally: one, two, three – oh my God, have I just pushed Jack too far? My heart is pounding and I may pass out at the thought that I may lose him again. Jack, please say something, I beg him in my head.

Jack takes my face between his big palms and searches my eyes, but I can see that he's trying to search my soul. Time goes still while I wait for my future with the man I love to unfold before me or to slip through my fingers.

"I'll be damned for my stupidity but I want to trust you. Christ, I need to."

I exhale the breath I'd been holding and sigh in relief. Jack's hands fall to his sides and he takes a step back. I reach a hand out for him, but he shakes his head. "Go now, Lisa, before I change my mind. I'm only human."

I hold back my tears, yet again amazed by the strength and the sensibility of this man. I still can't believe that he chose to share the deepest, most private side of himself with an ordinary girl like me. There's one thing I can see crystal clear: I may never deserve him, but I'll spend my life trying. "I won't let you down, baby, you'll see," I say vehemently.

"I'll be waiting for you here. Just come back when you're done," he says.

I stall there for a moment. This is it, this is what unconditional trust looks like.

Now go and earn it, Lisa.

I take the elevator down and all but run for the door. I hail a taxi and jump in it, blurting out Nico's address. I can't wait to be back in Jack's arms.

***

"It stinks in here. Why have you started to smoke again? It's bad for your voice," I say, snatching the unlit cigarette hanging from Nico's mouth away from his lips. They curve in a dejected smile.

"I don't care. Me and the guys split up."

"Why?" I ask in shock.

"We tried, but it wasn't the same without Lallo. I could never replace him anyway. The band just died without him."

"I'm sorry, Nico. What are you gonna do now?"

"I don't know."

"Is this what you wanted to talk about?" I ask gently. He looks exhausted, worn out. He shakes his head and drops himself onto the couch next to me.

"What happened to you? Are you ill?"

"Do you remember Kate?"

How could I forget that brat? "Yes," I say, my brows arching. "What about her?"

Nico rubs his eyes. "She's five months pregnant."

"What?" I ask in disbelief.

"She told me this morning. By text," he says in disgust.

Oh, my God.

"She's pregnant? But how did you   I mean, you always, you know, use protection." I hate that my cheeks burn but there's nothing I can do about that. Despite our history together, it just feels awkward now that I'd know something so intimate about Nico.

"My Lisa, always the practical girl," he says. His eyes fill with regret and his lips curve in the saddest smile I've ever seen. "I was drunk."

I try to contain my shock: Nico doesn't need to see it. This is already difficult enough for him. I lock my hands in my lap and wait in silence while he collects his thoughts.

"I can't believe that something like that happened to me. It's so surreal."

It is indeed. Nico is hot-headed but he'd never put himself at risk like that. And then it hits me. "It happened at your birthday party, didn't it? When you two disappeared together?"

He nods, avoiding my gaze.

"Oh, Nico." My racing heart slams against my ribcage. Nico was drunk, but Kate wasn't. When she dragged him to the restrooms, he could barely stand, but Kate's eyes were clear, her smirk sharp. I will always remember that she aimed both at me. She knew the risk she was taking. Does Nico know that?

He threads his hands through his tousled hair. "You told me she was bad news. Lallo tried to warn me as well, but no, I had to fall into her petty trap. How could I let my child be conceived in the stinking toilet of a club? How could I let that happen?"

He springs up and starts to pace the room. "She waits five months. Five. Months," he says, spreading his long fingers right in my face, "before she even tells me, because she needs to get 'her head around it.' And guess what? Now she doesn't want to keep my child! She wants to give my baby boy away for adoption! Can you believe that? Why are you smiling now?" he asks, frowning.

"You just called Kate's baby 'your baby boy.' Your baby's lucky, Nico. It doesn't matter how your child was conceived. You'll make a terrific dad."

Nico stares down at me with wide eyes. He comes to sit down back next to me and skims his knuckles over my cheek. "It should have been you. You should have been the mother of my children, after we got married. We should have been a family."

He's looking beyond my shoulder. Is he imagining how I would have looked like with his child on my hip? "No, Nico. There was a time when I believed that we had a future, but I wasn't seeing clearly."

"I still think we would have been good together, but it doesn't really matter now, does it?"

"No, it doesn't."

Nico nods. "I didn't think your boyfriend would let you

come to my place. If I'd been him, I wouldn't have. Does he even know that you're here?"

I give him a look.

"Are you… does he make you happy?"

"He's the best thing that has ever happened in my life," I say sincerely.

"Come here," he says. He wraps me in a tight hug. I stiffen and then sigh in relief: this is a friend's hug. "I want you to know that I'll always be there for you, Lisa. I know I hurt you in the past, over and over again, but if he doesn't treat you as you deserve, you know where you can find me," Nico says in my hair.

I smile against his shoulder, a huge weight lifting from my shoulders. I don't need Nico anymore. A sense of peace sets deep inside of me. Life is a long sequence of cycles and the one when Nico and I behaved as a man and a woman has just closed. A new time is starting right here and now: the time when our friendship will lead our thoughts and actions.

"Thank you for listening and for believing I can be a good father. Just… for everything."

"That's what friends are for."

"I guess so."

"Thanks to you, too."

"For what?"

I grin up at Nico. "For making me an aunt."

***

I fly down the stairs of Nico's building and all but launch myself into a cab. The taxi driver turns to give me an annoyed look. I shrug my shoulders. I don't want to be one more minute apart from the man of my life.

I call Jack to let him know that I'm on my way, but my call goes into voicemail; I leave a brief summary of my meeting with Nico and hung up. Impatient to hear his voice, I try his mobile again after a few minutes, but he's not picking up. Panic seizes my breath: did I take too long? Has Jack changed his mind about us?

The screen of my phone flashes in the darkness of the car.

Jackson: Meet me at Origami at 8pm

Oh! I give Origami's address to the taxi driver. He mutters under his breath: Chelsea is on the opposite direction to where we were going.

I clench my phone. Why doesn't Jack want to meet with me at his place? All sorts of bad scenarios parade in my head until I decide that I need a reality check. I speed-dial Penny's number and she answers immediately.

"How did it go?" I smile: always straight to the point, Penny.

"Great. Nico's gonna be a daddy."

"Whaaat?" Penny screams in my ear.

"I'll tell you more later."

"Where are you?"

"In a cab, heading for Origami."

"Yummy!"

"I was supposed to meet Jack back at his place but he texted me to meet him at the restaurant, instead. Maybe I shouldn't have gone to Nico. Maybe Jack's fed up with me trying to redefine my relationship with my ex. I wouldn't blame him."

"Chica, please, don't doubt yourself like that! Ah, women! Why do we always have to question ourselves like this? Just think about it, Lisa: what man invites his girlfriend to one of the best restaurants in London to dump her?"

"Well, maybe Jack would. He's a gentleman. I don't know. I'm confused."

"Lisa, do you want to be with Jack?"

"There's nothing I want more."

"Then you've got to give him credit and believe that he just wants to treat you to your favorite food."

I squeeze my eyes shut. "I'll try."

"Call me later, when you're happily stuffed with sushi. Hasta luego."

Maybe Penny is right. Maybe I'm worrying too much. I sit back and for the rest of the ride, I count the minutes that separate me from Jack.

Half an hour later, I pay the cabbie and step into the quiet foyer of Origami. Mrs. Kobayashi looks up from behind the small reception desk and I mirror her bow impatiently. "He's already here," she says, smiling, and gestures for me to go ahead into the restaurant.

I glance around and blink. The place is empty. How is it possible that one of the most sought-after dinner venues in London is empty on a Wednesday night? And then it hits me: today is Origami's closing day. I know for sure from when I tried to book a table for me and my mum. Did Jack ask Mrs. Kobayashi to open the restaurant only for us tonight? At least, if he wants to leave me, I won't be dumped in public. I cringe.

Jack walks up to me and stops right in front of me.

"You're smiling," I say in surprise.

"I am, baby. Is that bad?"

I shake my head. "I just thought… that you didn't want me at your place."

"Why on earth would you think that?" he asks, bemused. "It's quite the opposite, actually." He takes my hand and gently tugs me towards a table right in the middle of the small room. It's the only table set, I now notice. Always the gentleman, he pulls my chair out for me. I fall unceremoniously onto it, both exhausted by the long day and relieved that my boyfriend isn't mad at me. Penny's right. I worry too much. Jack stifles a chuckle and kisses the top of my head, then sits in front of me.

Mrs. Kobayashi brings two big plates of sushi to our table.

"I hope you don't mind that I've already ordered. They didn't have much left in the kitchen tonight, anyway. It's closing day," he says, filling my plate.

"Of course not. Thank you."

I take a big breath and dig into my dinner. "Did you get my voicemail?" I say, swallowing.

"I did."

"You can ask me anything you want, Jack. Anything: I've nothing to hide, I swear."

"I appreciate it, baby, but there's nothing I want to ask. All I need to know is that you're here with me now. That's all that matters."

"Oh, Jack." My vision blurs. "I don't deserve you."

"Oh, but you do, baby. I told you once that I wasn't looking for a perfect woman. Nobody is perfect. Look at me: I almost lost you when I moved to New York. How stupid was that?" he says, huskily.

"I love you so much, Jack," I whisper.

"I love you too, baby."

"So you're saying you love me even though I'm far from perfect?" I say, sniffing. Yes, maybe I'm fishing for a compliment; all girls do once in a while, don't we?

"I'm saying that you're perfect for me. That it's not about never making mistakes but how you learn from them. What I learned since I came back to London is that I'm never gonna let you go, ever again. I will take very good care of you, Lisa. Will you let me?"

"Of course," I say, beaming between tears.

"Let me start right now then," he says. He fishes a silver, rectangular box from the pocket of his jacket and pushes it to me across the table.

"What is this?" I ask in surprise.

"Just open it," he says, shifting on his chair.

I take the box in my trembling hands and open the lid. "A key?"

Jack's expression turns sober and he clears his voice. "Lisa, I'd give you the key to my heart but you stole it from under my nose the first time I met you. This is the key to my apartment. Will you move in with me?"

I stifle a chuckle.

"What's so funny?" he asks in a mix of confusion and horror.

"Did you rehearse what you've just said, baby?"

"Maybe," he says, glancing at me sideways.

I pinch myself. I mean, I put the key down and literally pinch myself. Jackson Kendall, American hunk, Harvard graduate, big shot at Remington, Gibson & Partners, sensual salsa dancer, sushi lover, but above all, the kindest and most thoughtful man I'd known, wants me to move into his place. Oh, and he actually rehearsed how he was going to ask me.

"What are you doing?" he asks, bemused,

"I'm just making sure I'm not dreaming."

"Is that a yes?" he asks hopefully.

I spring up, rush around the table, and launch myself into his waiting arms. "Si, si, si, amore mio, one hundred million times yes!"

EPILOGUE - Jack

Caleb drops down onto the sun chair next to mine. "All set."

"Thanks, man."

"Are you sure you wanna go ahead with this?"

I slide my sunglasses over my head and turn to my best friend.

"Don't give me that look, dude. Remember? You promised that when the day would come, you'd ask me twice, and I promised I'd do the same for you."

That makes me smile. "We were nineteen, Caleb."

"All the same."

I look out at the Mediterranean sea: it's cobalt blue and emerald green today, and 'as flat as oil,' as they say here in Italy. "She's a keeper, man. She's under my skin."

"She surely is."

I don't ask Caleb what part he agrees with: Lisa being worth keeping or her being under my skin. I'm well beyond that today. But back then…

When I moved back to London to stay with Lisa one year ago, Caleb told me to my face that it would be the biggest mistake of my life; that she would betray me again, and destroy me. As you can imagine, I didn't take it too well, coming from my best friend and all. But I understand now that he was worried about me. After all, I had given up a promotion to move back to Europe to stay with a girl who had slept with somebody else. Who in their right mind would have done that?

A man in love. And one experienced enough to discern if the lady is a cheater acting in bad faith, or if she's just a human being who made a one-off mistake. Believe me, I would have gladly made without the cheater earlier in my life, but that nasty experience turned out useful in the end. Every cloud has a silver lining. That's what Lisa does to me: she gives sense to everything in my life, past, present and future.

So I listened to my gut, and thirty-six hours after I'd made up my mind, I was touching down on British soil.

I've never looked back.

It took a while for Caleb to accept my decision, and to this day, I don't think he fully understands it. I wouldn't expect many people to, anyway. The sea is full of fish: that's more my best friend's kind of thinking. But when you find the One, that's it for a guy like me: priorities shift naturally and smoothly into their new order in your life, because that woman makes your life better. And God knows Lisa does.

She's my girl, my lover, my friend. Her love warms me and makes me feel alive like I've never felt before. Every day is different with Lisa: the closest thing to a lie she's ever told me is that she's boring. She sprinkles my life with tenderness and bliss. With her I've learned what friendship is really about, and, over time, I've also learned to trust again. This may not work for others but it surely does for me.

She emerges from the pool like a siren: her tanned skin glistens in the Italian summer sun, water dripping from her body, and I can't wait to put my hands and my mouth on her. I shouldn't have bought that skimpy red bikini: it's way too sexy on her. She's ravishing.

She twists her long, blond tresses and little drops fall over her full, half exposed breasts. I shift in my sun chair and look up. She's looking back at me, enjoying my reaction, the vixen. I make a mental note to return the teasing later. Lazy, creative summer afternoons spent with Lisa in the fresh shadows of our room have become my favorite pastime over the last week.

She walks to me, barefoot, and I don't miss the accentuated swing of her hips. Oh, she knows me so well.

"Don't," I say.

She smiles sweetly and drops on my lap. I absorb the delicious shock of her cold, wet skin against mine and wrap my arms around her body. She smells of apple and sun cream. "You're gonna pay for this, you know that, don't you?" I whisper in her ear.

"I really hope so."

I stifle a groan before Caleb tells us to get a room. Oh, we will. Later.

Lisa snuggles against me, like a kitten, like she always does.

She says it's her place, here against my chest, and I couldn't agree more. We belong together.

She doesn't know yet, but today, on Saint Lawrence night, I'm gonna ask her to marry me. She says stars will fall tonight, and I couldn't think of a more ideal setting for my wish to come true. I've wanted to ask her to be my wife for such a long time, well before it would have been wise. When I saw her eyes mist at Monique and Andy's the day he proposed, I decided that Elisabetta Castelli would be my wife, for good and for bad. And now it's time to make my move.

"Ragazzi e ragazze, il pranzo è pronto!" Lisa's mother calls from the door of our rented villa. My mum is standing next to her, skimming her hands over her white and yellow apron, smiling broadly. Who would have known? My mum and Lisa's have become friends. They don't understand much of what the other says, but they enjoy watching each other cook.

I slap Caleb on the back. "Instead of asking me stupid questions, what about you?"

"I'm working on it, my friend," he says, giving Denise a once-over. "I'm working on it. Just sit back and watch me."

Thank you for reading Silly Heart. If you enjoyed my book, please consider leaving a review

Here's how you can get in touch with me:
By **email**: alessandra@alessandramelchionda.com
On **Facebook**: www.facebook.com/a.melchiondawriter
On **Twitter**: @AleMelchionda
Would you like to watch videos of my books? Check out my **YouTube** channel:
http://www.youtube.com/alessandramelchionda
You can also check out my **website**: http://www.alessandramelchionda.com or read about me on my **Amazon** Page: amazon.com/author/alessandramelchionda or on my **Goodreads** Page:
http://www.goodreads.com/author/show/6903779.Alessandra_Melchionda

6122979R00123

Printed in Germany
by Amazon Distribution
GmbH, Leipzig